Refuel

A One Night Stand Bad Boy Romance

Pierce Motors
Book 1

Chiquita Dennie

304 Publishing Company

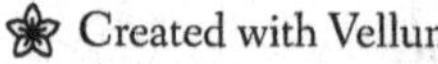 Created with Vellum

Grab some wine and get ready for more spicy, sinful, sexy suspense.

Are you signed up for my newsletter?

Join today and find out all the latest in new releases, contests, giveaways, sneak peeks and more.

www.chiquitadennie.com

Disclaimer

This work of fiction contains strong language and explicit sexual content and is only intended for mature readers. This story may contain unconventional situations, language, and sexual encounters that may offend some readers. If you're looking for sweet, fluffy romance, I would recommend another book. This book is for mature readers (18+).

Latest Releases

Latest Releases

Series

<u>Struck in Love</u>

The Early Years-A Prequel Short Story

Ruthless:Antonio and Sabrina Book 1

Savage: Antonio and Sabrina Book 2

Beastl: Antonio and Sabrina Book 3

Captivated By His Love:Janice and Carlo

Brutal: Antonio and Sabrina Booke 4

Redemption: Antonio and Sabrina Book 5

<u>Heart of Stone</u>

Broken, Book 1 (Emery & Jackson)

A Valentine's Day Short Book 1.5 Emery & Jackson

Rebirth, Book 2 (Jordan and Damon)

Reveal, Book 3 (Angela and Brent)

Bottoms Up Book 3.5 Jessica and Joseph Short

Renew, Book 4 (Jessica and Joseph)

<u>Cocky Billionaire Boys</u>

Cocky Catcher (Cocky Billionaire Boys Book 1)

Bossy Billionaire (Cocky Billionaire Boys Book 2)
The Fuertes Cartel
Stolen (The Fuertes Cartel Book 1)
Saved (The Fuertes Cartel Book 2)
Betrayed (The Fuertes Cartel Book 3)
Carrington Cartel
Torn: The Carrington Cartel Book 1
Claim: The Carrington Cartel Book 2
Something
Something Gained: A Romantic Comedy Book 1
Something Earned: A Romantic Comedy Book 2
Pierce Motors
Refuel: (Pierce Motors Book 1)
Pressure: Pierce Motors Book 2)
Summer Break
Summer Nights: (Summer Break Book 1)
TN Seal Security
Aydin: Book 1
Nasir: Book 2
Nicco: Book 3
Standalones
Until Serena(HEA World Novel)
Temptation
She's All I Need
I Deserve His Love
Mutual Agreement
Scoring with Sadie
Exposed (A Bodyguard Novel)
Love Shorts:A Collection of Short Stories
Red Light District(A Fantasy Romance Short)

Note From Author

This was originally published in 2020 as part of a fanfiction from Driven KB Worlds. Now the project is revamped and republished with new characters, but the same story of the racing world. I hope you enjoy it and continue to follow me for more updates.

Synopsis

Enjoy this steamy badboy, sports romance….

He's a badass driver on the race track, but then... so am I.

For one night, Arianna Pierce, allowed herself to be seduced and distracted, something she couldn't afford right now. But oh... was it worth every second and sensation. Breaking barriers as the first African American woman race car driver on her team, she's up against racing's top driver. Kamden "Kash" Coleman. He might have distracted her in bed, but on the race track, she's determined show him who's the boss.

Kash's life in rife with chaos. Ariana is a distraction and a pleasure he can't allow, whilst dealing with career pressures, problems with his ex, and the possibility that he might just become a dad. If he wants to prove his worth to his team, it's time to get his head in the race and his heart in the right place.

Refuel is a fast-paced, sexy, sports romance. You'll be scooped up into a world of

racing, whilst cheering on Arianna and Kash to not only win the race, but to win each other's hearts.

Character Interview: Arianna Pierce

Today, ladies and gentlemen, we have Arianna Pierce, a star driver for Pierce Motors, and cousin of billionaire racer car owner, Jackson Pierce, from Heart of Stone, sitting with us. We're discussing her journey in the latest release from author Chiquita Dennie. Welcome to our seventh installment of interviewing our characters. We look forward to many more and love hearing your questions.

Interviewer: So happy you've joined us today. I know you're a busy lady. I'll get right into the questions so fans can read about your journey. How do you feel about your story being told?

Arianna: The author promised my story would be authentic and true to my personality. Beyond thrilled for readers to check out my story.

Interviewer: How did Reece feel about your story?

Arianna: She was onboard and understood the ups and downs of finding love in public.

Interviewer: What would you say is the good and the bad of being a race car driver?

Arianna: Good is the power and adrenaline; bad is the paparazzi that constantly hound me.

Interviewer: So, are you saying the photographers are annoying?

Arianna: Yes.

Interviewer: I hear your story will cause readers to be on the edge of their seats.

Arianna: You never know what might happen.

Interviewer: Was it love at first sight?

Arianna: It was Vegas.

Interviewer: For readers who want to know if you've found love in this story, can you give us a hint?

Arianna: The readers will learn a lot about my life. Keep reading.

Interviewer: Can you give us more details on your plans for the future since we can't get any hints on your love life?

Arianna: My story may not end in just this book.

Interviewer: Can you give us a spoiler?

Arianna: Like they say, What Happens in Vegas Didn't Stay in Vegas.

Interviewer: Tell us your favorite race car driver besides yourself?

Arianna: Cyrus, of course.

Interviewer: I know I speak for all the readers today when I say that we appreciate you for hanging with us today. Readers enjoy, and let us know how Arianna fares in this new release.

Chapter One

Arianna

I held my palm up, covering my eyes and blocking the sun out. I blinked once, twice, and remembered celebrating with Essence and Reece last night. I looked down, noticing an arm across my waist, and I smirked. I looked over at the cutie, lightly snoring. I lifted his arm gently, moving it behind me as I eased out of the bed without making any noise. You would think the boy who had so much arrogance last night wouldn't look so innocent while he slept. The room was trashed with bottles of champagne, dishes from us ordering room service, and clothes. The second we walked into his suite, our clothes were tossed around as we devoured each other. The Venetian Hotel and Club was known for having high-profile guests and keeping transgressions out of the public. I grabbed my white slip dress off the floor, looking around for my bra and panties to put inside my purse. Peering under the bed, on top of the couch, and next to the window, I couldn't find them, so I decided to grab my clutch purse and heels to leave. Checking myself out in the mirror, I didn't look half bad for a girl who had a one-night stand. Deciding to leave a thank you note, I picked up the notepad and pen next to the bed and wrote *Thanks, Kash,* and placed it on top of the pillow for him to see. At first, he was an ass when he and his friends approached us, but my cockiness intrigued him. We ended up leaving to come up to his hotel suite.

All the women threw themselves at him, and I couldn't care less. It was about me enjoying myself with my girls and ultimately, the night turned out great and helped curb the six-month abstinence I unknowingly placed myself in from the lack of men I was interested in. Also, it didn't help having brothers, a father, and a cousin who constantly ran off any man who tried to get close. They felt I had terrible choices in men, and I could give them one or two men who broke my heart, but that's a part of life. Freddie broke up with me because of my family's interference. Malik and Eddison Jr., my older brothers, picked at him about everything and intimidated him for dating someone who came from a high-profile family, and that wasn't working. I couldn't help the fact that my cousin was Jackson Pierce, owner and CEO of Pierce Motors. The Pierce family didn't apologize for our excellence. My cell phone rang, and I removed it before it caused him to wake up, walked to the front door, and opened it slowly to avoid disturbing his sleep.

"Hello," I whispered, easing the door closed as the housekeeper smiled at me. I smiled back, removing the *Do Not Disturb* sign from the door. It was my idea to come to Vegas once I got word that my cousin, Jackson, agreed to let me try out as a rookie driver.

"I hope you used protection," Essence joked through the phone. I smelled my breath and underarms.

"Says the woman who made out with the waiter," I

replied, heading to the elevator and pressed the lobby button. It lit up as I stepped on.

"He looked like Michael B. Jordan. What can I say?" Essence commented as the door closed.

I laughed at her statement, seeing a reflection of myself through the closed doors. I gasped at the purple hickey on my neck.

"What's wrong?" Essence asked.

"Ughh... that jackass."

"Are you on your way to the lobby? Reece is freaking out," Essence inquired.

"Yeah."

Reece was my other best friend, and she was the one who kept us from getting into trouble most of the time. I was twenty-three and the youngest out of three kids, unmarried, and making six figures as the event coordinator of Cyrus Premier Enterprises and Pierce Motors. I looked just like my mom with long, thick, black hair that hung down my back along with thick, high-arched eyebrows, and heart-shaped lips. Also taking after my mom, I didn't smoke, only drank occasionally, ate semi-healthy, and worked out to maintain my size ten. I was muscular and soft at the same time with curves and hips, plus toned arms for kicking ass when I get disrespected. My dad put me in boxing classes when I was younger to learn how to protect myself in case he wasn't around, and I continued with the lessons even until this day.

"Finally!" Reece said.

I turned and saw Reece and Essence sitting in the lobby with turned-up lips and narrowed eyes. We had a private suite, thanks to Cyrus, her boyfriend—the owner of Cyrus Premier Enterprises I stayed with my new friend last night, so I knew they were probably worried that I should have come back to sleep in our room last night. However, Kash and I got distracted trying to compete to see who could make the other have the most orgasms. I lost, of course, but I did put him to sleep with a good mic session.

"Sorry, ladies, don't be mad. It couldn't be helped," I replied, hugging them both.

Essence sniffed me, and I pushed her off me.

"Eww, what are you doing?" I asked.

"Trying to see if you at least washed his scent off you," Essence stated as she pushed the revolving door of the front entrance, shoving my luggage over to me, and pulling her bag behind her. We had a flight to catch back home to L.A. so we could be at work, fresh for Monday. Normally on Sundays, we had brunch, and then I spent the rest of the day with my family. Seeing how exhausted I still was from last night, it was best if I went home and rested for two days.

"I hope it was worth it," Reece said, getting inside the limo. Cyrus spoiled us whenever we had a girl's trip. She tried to decline often, but Essence and I enjoyed the extra perks. Especially having a private jet instead of waiting in line like everyone else for two to three hours. The driver grabbed my luggage, and I slid inside next to her as Essence closed the door right behind me.

"A lady never tells, Reece," I said, checking the text messages from my parents. Chavonne asked what time I was coming tomorrow, and Eddison Sr. told me not to forget our monthly date night this week. One Wednesday out of the month, we'd continued our tradition of catching up on everything.

"You think he's pissed because you left without

leaving your number? Does he even know your name?" Essence questioned.

Mom: *Still coming, pumpkin?*

Me: *Sorry, I'm slammed with work.*

Mom: *Tell Cyrus you need a break.*

Me: *LOL! I'll see what Reece can do.*

The driver closed the trunk door, came around, and walked to the driver's side, putting the key in the ignition, and driving off. We chatted on the way to the airport while I returned messages back and forth with my mom.

I shrugged my shoulders, not caring if he was mad. Men did it all the time; we both knew what we wanted, and no expectations were voiced by either of us beyond last night. I rubbed the hickey again, thinking of how I'd need to double up on foundation to cover up, since I took after my father, skin-tone-wise—a smooth hue of deep copper with warm reddish undertones. I needed to make an appointment to get my hair braided this week and pinned up. I loved the products by Tiffany Renee since they were all natural haircare products, and she was donating them to the next charity event we planned on having at Cyrus Premier Enterprises.

A few minutes later, the limo pulled up to the private airstrip. I unbuckled and grabbed my purse in preparation to get out. The door opened, Reece stepped out, and I followed suit with Essence behind me.

"He'll be fine. Besides, what happens in Vegas..."

"Stays in Vegas," all three of us said at the same time as we walked up the stairs of the private jet Cyrus owned. I plopped down on the seat, preparing to buckle up. It normally took about forty-five minutes to get back home. I noticed a text message pop up from my ex-boyfriend Freddie. I wondered what he wanted, but if he was planning on trying to get back together, I wasn't in the same space anymore as far as relationships were concerned. Becoming a driver was my passion, and love was taking a backseat for now.

"Ughh…" I sighed, turning my phone off.

"Who was that?" Reece questioned.

"Freddie, wanting to talk. We haven't spoken in over seven months, and now he wants to talk," I confessed, which was the last time he and my brothers got into it at a family dinner. Supposedly, he was talking to the press about us getting married, and that was news to me when I never expressed I wanted to get married or have kids right now. The flight attendant came around with drinks and a tray of snacks from fruit to breakfast sandwiches and muffins. My stomach growled.

"Do you plan on talking to him?" Reece asked, taking a bottle of water from the stewardess.

"Can I get a towel and toothbrush?" I needed to freshen up before I ate.

"Of course," Evelyn, the flight attendant, said.

She had been a part of the longtime flight team for Cyrus, along with George, her husband. They reminded me of older parents, always looking out for us when we went away on trips.

"Thanks," I replied, shaking my head at Reece before I opened the bottle and took a sip.

"How do you think it'll play out when it hits the papers?" Essence asked.

"It was a friendly conversation at the club," I responded, grabbed the towel and toothbrush out of her hands before I stood, and headed to the bathroom.

"Don't forget to wash between your legs," Essence joked.

"Shut up, Essence!" I shouted from the back of the plane.

"You say friendly conversation, but the way you two were hugged up, and people took photos of you two, I can imagine the gossip blogs going crazy," Ree announced.

Looking in the mirror, I turned the water on, then washed my face, and brushed my teeth. She had a point; I could be a little reckless sometimes. One of the reasons my family could get a little overboard with things was because I tended to forget I came from a well-known family. I tried not to let that hold me back and worked toward my goals. At a knock on the bathroom door, I opened it, and Eve stood there with a pair of leggings and a long t-shirt from my luggage. I smiled and thanked her before continuing to wash up and change. I stepped out of the bathroom feeling ten times better, then got comfortable as the doors closed, and we prepared to lift off.

"It'll be fine. I doubt anyone really noticed it was me," I said, turning and looking out the window as the seatbelt sign came on.

* * *

Two hours later, I arrived home and dropped my luggage near the door, tired and exhausted from the day. I turned on my answering machine; the messages were mostly for interview requests and brands wanting me to partner up as a spokesperson. My two dogs ran toward me as Cicely, my housekeeper, walked around the corner with her hands on her hips. I grinned, noticing her attitude right off the bat. Cicely was my nanny when I was younger, so she was like a second mom to me. She went between my parents' house, mine, and my brothers' houses, making sure things were clean, there was food in the fridge, and she occasionally babysat for Eddison Jr.'s two kids.

"What now, old lady?" I asked.

"Call me old lady and see what happens." Cicely smacked me gently on the thigh.

"I didn't do anything," I commented, then picked up the remote to turn the TV on. It was only one in the afternoon, and I was ready for a nap.

"Your mom told me you're going tomorrow for dinner," Cicely said, sitting next to me. She was in her late sixties with grown kids and grandkids. She didn't have to work, but she wanted to stay on after her husband passed. Both families got along great. I even hired her granddaughter, Ciara, to help manage my social media to earn extra money while she was in high school. She always felt like a little sister to me, but I treated her more like an employee and sometimes that could backfire, but she'd done well, stayed focused, and committed to graduate and have a career as a publicist. Since I worked for Cyrus Premier Enterprises and would hopefully start racing one day, we could bring her on full time.

"I'm tired and need a break after this weekend. Plus, I have work early Monday. I'd rather not get caught up in long conversations about how I'm living my life," I confessed, rubbing the back of Lucky and picking up Dreamy, my two Maltipoos. Cicely had a long streak of gray hair and still wore high heeled shoes at her age and stayed stylish, thanks to my family constantly spoiling her. We tried to get her to retire and travel the world, but she refused and always said there was nothing for her to see unless Billy, her late husband, was with her to see the world, too.

"Did you have fun?" Cicely questioned. I nuzzled up close to Lucky, lifted my eyes at her question, and smiled.

"Oh, Lord," Cicely said, dramatically throwing her hands up in prayer.

I busted out in laughter.

"Don't worry. I protected myself, Cicely. You worry too much, just like Mommy," I said, sitting up and turning the station to RuPaul's Drag Race.

"I'll end up having a heart attack dealing with you, girl," Cicely stated.

I leaned my head on her shoulder, getting comfortable.

"Did you cook?" I asked.

"You know not to ask that question. I always have something cooked for my babycakes," Cicely said, tapping my leg so she could get up. She walked off toward the kitchen, and I followed behind, with Lucky and Dreamy barking at each other. I adopted them two years ago, and they reminded me of my brother, Malik, and me constantly bickering. He was the best big brother in the world and spoiled me rotten. Also, he was the first person to tell me how I should be living my life, even though he was quick to yell out he was single and could date or do whatever because he was a man. I called bullshit every time, and our parents ignored us at this point when family dinners started up. It was the main reason I was avoiding dinner tomorrow.

Cicely grabbed the plate and a set of tongs, picking up pieces of roast, veggies, and salad. I put Lucky on the floor then washed my hands. I slid a glass under the ice machine and pushed hot water on the screen. It was an upgrade I had installed that automatically gave me puri-fied water to cut down on plastic bottles in the house.

Once I finished my lunch, I went to my room, turned the shower on, and grabbed something comfortable to sleep in since I was in for the rest of the day. I freshened up on the plane, but I could still smell him on me. Testing the water, I felt it wasn't the right temperature, so I picked up a hair clip to keep my hair out of the way while it heated to my desired preference. Once it was ready, I stepped inside, then grabbed my washcloth, and lathered it with my favorite coconut and lavender body wash to clean the weekend away.

* * *

Sunday

Grunting in annoyance, I felt the covers get pulled back and the curtains open, letting the sunlight get inside.

"Get out!" I shouted, pulling the blanket back over my head.

"No, it's noon, and you need to get up and get dressed," my cousin's wife, Emery, said.

"Is she up yet?" I heard another voice yell out before they walked into my bedroom with a plate that smelled like Cicely made her famous double cheeseburgers on avocado toast.

"Who invited you two in here?" I questioned, still under the covers.

"Reece told us about your little weekend of fun, and Auntie Chavonne was going to come over here until we said we would check on you," Emery told me.

"Emery, you're the last person who should be giving me advice on one-night stands," I replied, causing Essence to choke on her food while Emery just waved me off.

"For your information, I'm not here to give you

advice, only to check up on you so Jackson doesn't get involved."

"Why would he get involved? I'm twenty-three, an adult who owns her house, pays her own bills, and might I add, has a job."

"Yes, but you were acting reckless in Vegas, and I do remember two years ago, how you flew off to Europe so you could go find yourself. Jackson thinks of you like a little sister, and you've been wanting to get into the driving side of the business, correct?" Emery asked, and I tilted my head, knowing this was the biggest issue with my family, not supporting my dreams.

"Go put some clothes on, nasty," Essence said, sitting on the edge of the bed.

"Do you pay bills here?" I asked.

"No, but you have company, so get dressed," Essence responded.

"Ugh, you get on my nerves," I replied before I jumped up, stomped over to the closet to grab a pair of jeans and t-shirt to get dressed in the bathroom.

"Where's Reece?" I questioned from the other side of the bathroom door.

"She's with Atlas somewhere," Emery answered.

"What do you have planned for today? I'm not going to family dinner. I'm tired and want to relax in my home," I said, checking my messages.

Emery and Essence followed me out of my bedroom and down the hall to the kitchen. Cicely was doing the "Electric Slide", and I chuckled. When I purchased my place, she decided that on Sundays, she'd cook a big lunch and dinner, so I could just imagine what she had set up for today. I lifted the lid and smelled the spices of onions, garlic, and oregano bubbling in the pot of stew.

Taking the wooden spoon out of her hand, I tasted the flavors and closed my eyes, ready to stare at the food.

"This tastes so good," I said, rubbing my stomach.

Essence took a seat on the island, finishing her bowl of stew. Turning to the fridge, I grabbed a can of ginger ale then sat next to her.

"Emery, how are the kids doing?" Cicely questioned.

"They're good and spoiled, thanks to Jackson," Emery chuckled, standing against the island with her arms crossed.

"I know JJ wants me to pick him up for the weekend. I might bring all the kids over for a party," I said.

"That's fine with me. Keep them for the week if you want. So, tell me about this weekend?" Emery queried.

Cicely placed a bowl in front of us with spoons and napkins.

"Are you heading out for the day?" I inquired as I cut a piece of cornbread.

Cicely strolled about, nodding as she moved out of the kitchen to leave. I shifted in my seat, scooping carrots and corn together with cornbread.

"You know Malik will have something to say about this Vegas trip," Essence stated.

"Malik is my brother, not my father. Eddison Jr. is starting to learn to leave me alone," I sassed as I waved her comment off.

Emery was older than me and worked at Pierce Motors on the marketing side, on top of being a wife and the mother of four kids. I admired how she navigated her situation with Jackson; they started off from a one-night stand. But I wasn't looking for a relationship. I liked being single and able to date whoever I wanted.

"Well, I can't stay, and Jackson wanted me to check to

see if you were setting up a new charity event this year?" Emery wondered as she looked up from her vibrating phone.

"Send me the details. I must meet with Cyrus because he wants to do something with Cyrus Premier Enterprises. Maybe I can combine the events," I suggested before I wiped my mouth with the napkin on the table.

"Okay, lady, call me later once you rest up. I see the bags under your eyes now," Emery commented before she headed out, leaving me and Essence alone.

"Spill the real tea now that everyone left," Essence demanded.

"Nothing to tell; it was a one-time thing. I never back-track, Essence," I joked as I flipped her off. After we finished eating lunch, we watched movies for the rest of the day until she left. Then I worked on some ideas for charity events at CPE and Pierce Motors.

Chapter Two

Kamden

onday

As the driver headed toward the office of Cyrus Premier Enterprises, I wore my dark shades to avoid the sun. I was still hungover from the weekend in Vegas with my boys. I got an early morning call from my publicist; the management wanted to talk with me about some things. I didn't know what I did this time and didn't care. When it was my own time and not a CPE function, I was doing me at all times. I remembered waking up alone in bed for the first time since I became Kamden *Kash* Coleman, a professional Formula One driver. Life hadn't been the same, and women threw themselves at me. *Do I enjoy the comfort of women? Hell, yeah.* So, a few of my friends and I went out to Vegas to celebrate after I won a race. Bellevue Hotel provided a suite, and a new club section opened. I had two VIP sections roped off Friday night, and I took the offer. Being a celebrity often came with drawbacks, and then there were moments when the owners wanted you to be seen in their business to bring awareness that they catered to celebrities. Now to confess, waking up with a note on a pillow that said *Thanks* did piss me off, not a little, but a lot. Could I be a little cocky and arrogant? Yeah, and I wouldn't apologize when I came from nothing and worked hard to get where I was as the highest paid race car driver in the industry. People called me the playboy; I called it being single, and the women knew what they were getting.

The car stopped in front of Cyrus Premier Enterprises , and I opened the door, not waiting for the chauffeur. I might be cocky, but my mom did instill respect as a single mom raising a hot-headed boy. Despite my millionaire status at twenty-five from various endorsements and sponsorships, I was still humble about the way I grew up and saw it all from not having food to eat at times or staying home alone while Mom worked to pay bills. Going to school in secondhand clothes from thrift stores. When I turned fifteen, I got involved with the wrong crowd, stealing cars, and getting into fights. My parents never married, and my father walked out when I was younger, around five or six. My mom was worried I'd end up on the streets, so she pushed me into volunteering at a local center called The All Hands Home. They dealt with foster boys, and I hung around to help mentor the younger kids. I eventually started racing for fun and hooked up with Cyrus and Cyrus Premier Enterprises.

"Hey, Kash!" Sherah, Cyrus's secretary, greeted.

I waved and entered his office, not waiting for a command, and pulled my shades off before lying back on the sofa. He chuckled before telling whoever was on the other end of the phone that he would need to call them back. A second later, the loud voice of my manager and publicist for Cyrus Premier and Pierce Motors, Sarai Lambert, came inside.

"Have you lost your mind?" Sarai shouted.

I opened one eye at Sarai and smiled. She rolled her eyes in annoyance, with her jaw clenched. Reggie's eyes slightly narrowed. I laughed, crossed my arms behind my head, and whistled. Sarai was a beautiful woman, but I never looked at her as anything except a big sister at twenty-eight years old. Sarai had an old soul and was quick to tell you what you needed to hear and not what you wanted to hear.

"Calm down, Sarai, you're giving me a headache," I said and felt a thump across my forehead.

"You're giving me one too, Kamden," she replied, calling me by my first name. Only my closest friends and family called me Kamden. The rest of the world knew me as Kash. Figuring I wouldn't win the battle, I sat up, arms stretched on top of the couch.

"What did I do now?" I questioned, and Reggie tossed magazines on top of the desk with me plastered across, hugging up with the girl from the nightclub. Well, this time my antics might have been blown out of proportion. I knew of Pierce Motors and Jackson being the owner. We'd collaborated a few times on some charity work and interviews. Seeing me hugged up with his cousin might not play well and cause more spotlights aimed on my personal life instead of my career.

"Sorry."

Sarai opened and closed her mouth, then grunted in frustration.

Cyrus leaned forward in his chair and in a controlled voice, he said, "All right, guys, give him a little breathing room. He's still learning. Look at me and how I started out before Reece walked into my life."

"See," I said and pointed between us. Cyrus motioned for me to be quiet.

"Cyrus, I'm not babying him. Arianna is the daughter of Eddison Pierce and the cousin of Jackson Pierce. Do you know how big of a scandal this can get if we don't handle this early enough?" Sarai commented.

"Did you use protection with her?" Reggie questioned.

I nodded, and all three relaxed, letting out long-held breaths. There was a knock on the door, and Sherah came in, not waiting for anyone to call her inside.

"Cyrus, I brought some coffee for everyone. Especially your favorite espresso shot with whipped cream, Kash," Sherah expressed, bending down in front of me, showing off her cleavage in a low-cut, button-up, white blouse and red skirt that was so tight, I could see the imprint of her thong. I forgot to mention I did sleep with Sherah once, and she'd only gotten even more obsessed with wanting to become an actual couple. Cyrus warned me not to mess with employees, but at twenty-five, one hundred ninety pounds, and height around five-ten, my smile was the first thing that drew women to me and possibly my slick comments. Mary Coleman said the first thing I did when I was a baby was smile at the nurse when I was born, and nothing was ever the same.

I winked at her, picking up the shot and throwing it back. "Thanks." Sarai paused, looked at Sherah, then shook her head.

"This is why I want to quit every week, Cyrus," Sarai muttered, sitting in the chair in front of his desk. He passed a pile of documents to Sarai.

"That will be all, Sherah," Cyrus said, and she twitched her hips, leaving the room.

"Kash, you need to take things more seriously. Do you want to continue down this path of sleeping around with random women?" Reggie called out. I met Reggie about three years ago at a charity ride, and Cyrus introduced us. He was looking for a fresh face. He was a much older man who wanted me to settle down and stop partying so much. I waved everyone off and stood.

"Is this meeting all about my love life? I'd rather get to the lane and run some laps," I answered, peering from Reggie to Sarai. Cyrus never jumped on the bandwagon and gave his advice when we were alone.

"You're not racing today, Kamden. We have photographers outside interviewing her for Sunday's upcoming race. I don't need things getting off track because she showed up, stealing the limelight," Sarai implied.

"That hurts my feelings, Sarai."

"Good," Sarai answered.

"So, what do you propose I do? It was a one-night stand, and she left before I could get her last name that morning."

Sarai gasped and raised her hand to her chest in shock.

"Are you saying you slept with a woman who ditched you?" Sarai asked with a mischievous smile.

I stuck my middle finger up as she bent over laughing.

"I wasn't looking for her last name, so it doesn't matter," I responded.

"This could go one of two ways, Kash. If you lay low for a few weeks and stop hanging out at clubs, blogs will find something else to talk about, or a media storm will erupt if you two continue dating," Reggie stated.

"Who said I wanted to date her?" I asked.

"It doesn't matter if you want to date her or not. Arianna works at Cyrus Premier Enterprises throwing events. We need people focused on your career, not your love life," Sarai reminded me.

I swallowed a lump in my throat. Sarai was right, and I hated to admit it and give her credit. My career was the most important thing to me. Many times, I'd seen careers go downhill when the media attached a driver with a celebrity.

"I promise she's not on my mind, and I'll stay away," I replied as I headed toward the door.

"Where are you off to now?" Cyrus asked, clasping his hands together.

"To get cleaned up and down to the locker room. I'll stay out of the way. Promise, Sarai."

Opening the door and leaving, out the corner of my eye, I watched as Sherah licked her lips while on the phone, and I motioned for her to follow me to the private bathroom. Sherah hung up the phone and jumped up, giggling, before looking back to make sure the door was closed. I placed my finger to my lips to stay quiet, glancing around the office to make sure no one was around.

"I thought it was a one-time thing, Kash?" Sherah questioned while unzipping her skirt. I raised my hand to stop her.

"No, leave your skirt on. We don't have time for that with me needing to get down to practice. Help me out to take the stress away with your pretty lips around my dick," I said, caressing her cheek. I told them I'd stay away from Arianna Pierce, but I didn't mention anything about other women. Sherah grinned, walked out of my arms, and locked the door. She dropped to her knees, unzipping my jeans, and helped take the stress away.

* * *

An hour later, I walked in the garage and heard music blasting as the crew prepared the car for today's run. I wasn't planning on doing anything but getting some rest. Now that it was out in the public and the news media ran the story, I couldn't let my reputation get drowned out with conversations about a love life that didn't exist.

"Look what the dead woke up," Tripp chuckled as he held out his right hand for me to shake. I pushed it away and stepped around him to check the board of who was up to practice first. Tripp worked for Cyrus Premier Enterprises and was one of my best friends from Fresno. He was a little taller than me at six-three in height, around two hundred and thirty pounds with long, blond hair that he kept in a ponytail on the top.

"How long has the media been here?" I raised my hand and removed my sunglasses.

Tripp glanced up and over toward the makeshift interview in the middle of the track.

He pushed his fingers through his hair. "Since around eight this morning, and it's now going on eleven. I wish they'd leave," Tripp replied.

"Damn, I guess I'll stay out of the way." My brow scrunched in a frown.

"The gossip is running around saying you got married. Then Josie came looking for you," Tripp casually mentioned.

"Shit, I forgot about Josie wanting me to take her out."
A thin smile edged his lips.

"The real question is why you continue dealing with her," he said.

"Kash! Kash! Are the rumors true?" a reporter called out, and I decided it was time for me to get out of dodge before Cyrus heard about this.

I threw my shades back on and dapped fists with Tripp before sliding out the side door toward my car to head home and prepare for my upcoming race.

Chapter Three

Arianna

I stood at the window of Pierce Motors prepared to talk with my cousin when I glanced and saw the cars drafting around the track. I saw number twenty-five almost spin out of control, but he recovered the wheel in time.

I walked into Jackson's office with Essence behind me as support. I wasn't leaving without an answer today and now that the news got out with photos of me in Vegas, I needed to make my case for why I deserved a spot as a driver.

"Hi, cousin," I said, walking forward. I wore my best suit and had my hair freshly braided up in case I got to do a few laps. Jackson glared, put the newspaper down on his desk, and tapped his finger on the call button. I was already imagining the attitude I'd end up dealing with, but I tried to avoid him until it was necessary.

"I wanted to talk alone," I said.

He pointed at Essence standing next to me.

"Essence doesn't count," I commented, and Jackson grunted.

"Where is she?" I heard Malik call out over the intercom.

"Calm down, Malik. Come to my office if you can control your temper," Jackson reminded him.

Essence patted my shoulder for moral support.

"Fine," Malik stated.

"You're the talk of the town, Arianna. Not for the right reasons I must say." Jackson was older and considered me a little sister. At least he gave me breathing room to make mistakes, unlike my brothers and father.

"I know, and I apologize about that. I was celebrating with friends, and things got a little out of hand."

"More than out of hand, Arianna. You're on the front page with your tongue down Kamden's throat. *New York Style* is talking about you two as the new 'it' couple. They have you guys getting married and having kids secretly," Jackson fussed.

"Jackson, you know more than anyone how the media spins things," I answered, and the door popped open with Malik coming inside.

"I don't want to hear it, Malik," I said, ignoring his harsh glare.

"You need to hear because you're acting reckless, Ari." He called me by the nickname he gave to me when I was younger. He was the only one who got away with calling me Ari in our family and friends.

"Jackson, I want to race," I started, getting down to the point of this visit.

Malik and Jackson peered at each other, then burst into laughter.

Appalled, I jumped up with my hands on my hips and pointed my finger between the two.

"Arianna, you are not driving for Pierce Motors or any other team. It's too dangerous," Malik said.

"I'm talking to Jackson, the owner and CEO," I spat, then sighed at the disappointed look on Jackson's face.

"Arianna, you're too young to be racing," Jackson told me.

"I'm twenty-three, and most of your guys who race are twenty-one. So, that's no excuse, and you're only saying no because I'm a girl."

Malik shrugged his shoulders, and I stepped over, facing Jackson and blocking out Malik.

"Jackson, let me drive one time and see what I can do. Please, if I do a terrible job, I'll never mention it again."

"Let me think about it, but we need to discuss this situation with Kamden Coleman and you." Jackson brought up the scandal that had exploded across the media.

I knew who Kamden was when I decided to sleep with him, and I wasn't looking for anyone to tell me I was being stupid for doing what other single women did every day.

"My personal life is none of your business or Malik's."

"It is when your situation comes across my desk in a phone call from reporters and social media bringing up how my little cousin is pregnant and engaged before the family has even met this guy," Jackson explained.

"It was one night, Jackson, I can promise. Kash and I will probably never see each other again," I exclaimed.

"Arianna, you can't be serious. He races for Cyrus Premier Enterprises, which you work for part time," Jackson insisted.

"One race, and I'll forfeit my fee for the charity event," I threw in as an added bonus.

"Jackson, think about the publicity that can come to Pierce Motors with having a female driver, another African-American woman pushing the barriers," Essence implored on my behalf.

"Please, cousin, you're my favorite," I pleaded as I put my hands in prayer form.

"One race, Arianna," Jackson responded, and I jumped up screaming in joy.

I heard Malik groan behind my back.

"Yes! Thank you. I promise you won't regret this." I pulled him into a hug and kissed his cheek.

I clapped my hands and locked my right arm with Essence as we danced out of his office.

* * *

Two hours later, I was at my mom's house, and I called Reece and Sarai over to celebrate with Essence and me. My mom made margaritas, chips, salsa, and quesadillas. It was lunchtime and rather than heading back to the office, I decided to take the rest of the day off to prepare myself for what was to come.

"I can't believe Jackson agreed to let you race," Reece said.

I dipped my chip in the salsa, biting into the spices.

"Believe it, best friend, and you're going to help me practice," I said.

"What did Malik say again?" Mom quizzed, pouring sour cream on top of her chips and salsa. She set the patio up with food and drinks. Cicely was off today, and my dad was away at work as the head of acquisitions for Pierce Motors. Having the family involved in the industry helped me to get forward in the business, but working hard and going to school was another requirement before branching out on my own with my career.

"Tell me about this Kamden person," Chavonne commanded.

"He's cocky and rich, Auntie, and that's the best reason to see him again," Essence blurted out.

Chavonne tossed her head back, laughing at Essence's statement.

"Oh my god! Weren't you making out with some guy at the club, too?" Reece challenged, making Essence choke on her drink, so I patted her back.

"Yep, she sure did. Kash is sexy with a dangerous look about him that will have you drunk off his kisses. Tall, I think about five-nine or five-ten. I'm five-four, so it was the perfect combination, plus tattoos on his arm," I explained.

"Has dark, low-cut hair, wide nose, dark brows, deep-brown eyes, and he had one of those square jawlines and full lips," Essence ran down his list of attributes.

"Did you sleep with him or did Essence?" Mom chortled, motioning between us.

All three of us laughed at her comment.

"No, Auntie, your daughter had the pleasure of seeing all the glory of Kamden Kash Coleman," Essence spoke in an amused voice.

"Reece, what do you think about me driving for Pierce Motors opposite of Cyrus Premier Enterprises? You think Cyrus will be mad?" I questioned.

"No, he supports your dreams. Same as me. Just be careful; some people can be vicious. And I did hear that Kash has a few women he deals with, so make sure you don't fall in deep," Ree explained.

"That will never happen," I announced.

"Don't say I didn't warn you," Reece remarked.

Chapter Four

Arianna

Once lunch was over, Jackson called me to come up to headquarters to discuss his expectations of my first race. I pulled into the parking structure and turned my car off, taking the key out of the ignition. Removing my seatbelt, I sat back, taking in the venue and smiled at what I was preparing to do. When I was younger, I'd always wanted to get into racing, but my family felt I was caught up in the hype of the glamour and riches of being famous. In my eyes, driving was an escape for me. A path to release all the stress of the world and let it all fly away, to focus on point A to B. Racing was a male-dominated world. I knew this, but I would never let my dream fade from my mind. Even if Jackson declined, I'd find another way to get on a team.

"Ready," I whispered, opening the door and stepping out.

Reece and Essence came around to the driver's side as the paparazzi bolted toward me with flashes of cameras and microphones.

"Arianna Pierce, are you Kash Coleman's fiancée?" one reporter asked.

"What?" I screeched.

"Arianna, let us have the exclusive interview with you and Kash," a second reporter requested, and I pushed my way through the door.

"Nobody is getting married. Do your research, people," Essence chastised, yelling at the security to do something. I walked over to the elevator and scanned my badge as we stepped on.

"You think he changed his mind?" Essence asked.

"I hope not," I replied.

The elevator stopped on the twenty-fifth floor, and I stepped off, heading in the direction of his office. Waving to his secretary, I knocked on his door and waited for him to invite me in.

"It's open!" Jackson yelled.

I turned the knob, walked inside, and froze when I saw the person standing near the corner of the window.

"It's you," Kash said, giving me a hard stare.

"What is he doing here?" I questioned.

"Cyrus, what's going on?" Reece asked. I noticed him in the corner with a wide smirk on his face, along with Malik and my dad. I hoped this wasn't some type of intervention.

"Jackson called me because the media is getting out of hand with the reports on Kash and Arianna," Cyrus answered as he grabbed her in a hug, kissing her cheek.

"We saw them outside. Are they at Cyrus Premier Enterprises, too?" I inquired, running a hand up my arms, trying to keep my eyes off Kash.

"They are, and I know you want to race soon, but I'm thinking we need to wait," Jackson replied.

"Wait! She wants to race cars?" Kash inquired.

"Yes, I do, and the name is Arianna. I recall you calling it over and over again without any problems."

"Ari, we don't need to hear all that!" Malik shouted.

Kash licked his lips, not taking his eyes off me. I felt naked in his presence. Clearing my throat, I stated, "Uhm, Jackson, I want to go through with my race. It shouldn't change if you keep them in a certain area so as not to interrupt anything. This is my big chance."

"You guys can't be serious to allow a chick in a race," Kash remarked.

"They are, and it's none of your business what Pierce Motors does, Mr. Coleman."

"Kamden," Kash replied.

"What?" I questioned, taking in a sharp breath.

"Call me Kamden, like you were doing over and over again that night." His eyes raked over my body.

"Do you two need to be left alone?" Essence queried.

"No!" Malik and I said at the same time.

"Look, am I racing or not?" I demanded, panic swelling inside me.

"What do you think about this, Cyrus?" Jackson raised himself to his feet, sliding his hands in his pockets.

"If she wants to drive, I don't see why she can't. I'm all for anyone who wants to drive," Cyrus stated, and I released a breath as he winked at me.

"Cyrus, you know this is a dangerous sport," Kash informed him.

"You do it, so what's the difference?" I insisted as I stepped in front of him, closing the distance between us.

"Baby, I'm trying to keep that pretty little face of yours from getting scratched," Kash said, lifting my chin, staring into my eyes. I never noticed the way his eyes were completely black as he touched my chin. I wasn't sure if he was being sincere or trying to get me out of the way.

"Arianna, not baby," I blurted, removing his hand from my face.

He smirked and raised his hands in apology.

Essence pressed a hand to her mouth to stifle her giggles. "You two are cute. Make sure I'm the godmomma!" Essence said. I groaned at her statement as I turned around, remembering I wasn't alone.

My brow creased in anger. "Essence," I said as I glared at her.

"One race, you two stay away from each other, and maybe this mess will die down. Arianna, don't forget you still have a job to do with the charity event," Jackson stated as he gave out the rules.

"No worries; that won't happen again," I said.

"No doubt; it was a Vegas moment that stayed in Vegas," Kash agreed.

Malik sighed and walked out of the room with disappointment across his face. I knew we'd need to have a conversation later, but I was too excited to get started.

Cyrus headed out with Reece next to him, and I strolled out of Jackson's office. I felt an instant shock from someone grabbing my arm and pushing me up against the side corner of the wall, away from Jackson's office. Kash ran his thumb down my arm, up to my cheek before lifting my chin.

"What do you think you're doing, little baby?" Kash questioned.

"What are you talking about, Kash?"

"You knew who I was when we went to the hotel room. Is this some way to get back at your parents and brothers?" Kash asked.

"Don't flatter yourself, Kash."

He bit his bottom lip, leaning in close as his lips barely grazed mine.

"Call me Kamden, Ari," Kash answered.

I grimaced that he felt he had the right to give me a nickname and pushed him back to put a little space between us.

"The name is Arianna."

Kamden chuckled and held out his hand.

"Kamden Coleman. Nice to meet you officially, Arianna Pierce."

I stuck my hand out, letting it fall into his embrace. That same sheering shock from before spurred in my stomach, and I removed my palm, wiping it on my leg.

"Too hot for you," Kamden stated.

"No, my hands tend to sweat a lot."

"Racing. Do you think that's a good idea? I mean it can get dangerous, and I know how the guys act behind the scenes."

"Kamden, I'm not naïve. I grew up in this world. I can take care of myself."

The solid-wood door of Jackson's office flew open, and he stepped out, causing us both to separate.

"Arianna, I thought you left already," Jackson said.

"I was... I mean... I am," I answered.

"Kamden, get with Sarai when you have a moment so she can write up a joint statement. You two need to stay away from each other so this can go away," Jackson said.

A relieved look washed over his face, and I felt a certain way about how this was made out to be some mistake. Two consenting adults made a decision and had fun; no harm was done to anyone, and love was never a factor. *Why was my family fighting to bury a lie?* I thought to myself.

Catching up to Essence as Reece got in the car with Cyrus, I tapped on the window of his Ashton Martin before he could pull off.

"Cyrus, I'm still prepared to put on the charity event with Pierce Motors. I think a joint gathering would bring more press for both companies," I said.

"That's great, Arianna. Get with Reece and send me the details. You know money is no object," Cyrus stated as he turned over the ignition, honked, and drove off.

"Damn! I need to get a race driver," Essence announced.

"Essence, calm your hot pussy down," I joked as I pulled my key out of my pocket and inserted it in the driver's side door.

"Malik was pissed about you driving, plus your little boyfriend," Essence said, shutting the passenger side door.

"Kamden is not my boyfriend."

"The way your eyes lit up when you saw him in the office didn't fool me."

"Essence, any man who has a pulse is your type. Sorry if I don't take your advice on this subject."

Essence waved me off with her long dainty fingers.

Chapter Five

Arianna

One week later

I was in my office with Reece, creating a plan for the charity that Cyrus Premier Enterprises and Pierce Motors would be co-hosting. I still hadn't talked with my brother about me racing. I'd been avoiding his calls and text messages. It was always an argument of me being too young and not equipped to handle the life of a race car driver. I'd been training for years, and Cyrus had helped me to get where I needed to be, thanks to Reece putting in a good word for me.

"I like what you did with your office, Ari," Reece said.

"You do?"

"Yeah, it's your personality. Heather should do something like this to her office with the plants and vanity set."

"Thank you. I knew Cyrus when I worked here part time at CPE. I wanted something fresh, clean, but still cute. I got the silver and cream color scheme from some fashion magazine," I responded.

"Perfect touch of feminine and bossy," Reece declared.

"Which exactly explains my personality!" I announced in a snicker.

Reece sat in the chair in front of my desk and turned her body.

"By the way, Cyrus asked me if you're dating Kamden."

I swallowed a sudden dryness in my throat and stopped typing on my computer.

"Do you think it was stupid to sleep with him?"

"I think you knew what you were doing when you slept with Kamden," Reece informed me.

"Is this honest hour?" I inquired, using our calling card whenever one of us needed to talk about something serious.

"Spill it," Reece said.

I leaned back in my chair, closing my eyes, thinking back on the day of our time in Vegas. I had just wanted to get away from the noise and craziness of my ex, Freddie, constantly calling and texting.

"I liked him, and I had seen him a few times around Cyrus Premier Enterprises. He looked like a challenge with all the women around him, so I took a chance."

"So, this was more of a game for you?" Ree wondered.

I felt a lump at the back of my throat.

"No, of course not. Ree, you know me. Besides, he's the playboy who has multiple women on his arm."

"I can remember going through the same thing with Cyrus in the beginning. My advice is to make sure you know what you're doing and to not lead him on," Reece replied.

"I have no reason to contact Kamden beyond our little Vegas time; he doesn't have anything I want in an official boyfriend."

"I think he's single," Reece told me.

"Good for him."

Reece chortled as she said, "That sparkle in your eyes. You got it bad, Ari."

"I recall you falling all over yourself with Cyrus. Something about getting a little too close on the dance floor at a nightclub," I said.

"We're talking about you right now," Ree retorted.

"No, we're talking about this charity event. So, what do we want to do?" I asked.

"I was thinking of a charity ride with both teams."

"What about making the tickets a certain price, and they get a charity ride, then dinner with the drivers to the highest bidder?" I questioned.

"That sounds amazing," Ree answered.

I heard a knock on the door, and my secretary, Tisha, walked inside with a bouquet of flowers. It was a large, clear vase with yellow roses—my favorite color.

"Look what came today," Tisha announced.

I smiled, thinking my brother probably decided to finally give a peace offering.

"Those are gorgeous," Reece said.

"They were just delivered," Tisha answered.

I removed the card and smelled a very distinctive scent I couldn't place in my memory.

"Who are they from?" Reece questioned.

Opening the card, I turned it around and read the inscription.

Ari, I meant to say thank you for a lovely night, but you left without kissing me goodbye.

Kamden 'Kash' Coleman.

I looked up and noticed Tisha and Reece waiting for me to answer. Ripping the card up, I dropped it in the trash can and picked the flowers up, passing them back to Tisha.

"The flowers are for you, Tisha," I said.

"What!" Tisha said, surprisingly.

"Yeah, it's from Cyrus as a thank you for all your hard work," I lied, trying to get her out of my office. A confused expression came across her face.

Would I pursue anything with him? No. He was too cocky for me, and I'd probably end up brokenhearted. I didn't want to go down that road.

"I saw the note," Reece commented, taking a seat again.

I flushed in embarrassment.

"Note. What note?"

Reece pointed over to the trash can. I followed her eyes, sighing in annoyance.

"You don't have to tell me, but I can see your interest."

"The charity race is a good idea. Maybe we do five laps with signs of the charities displayed," I said, to change the subject.

"Mmm... Okay, we can change the subject this one time," Reece replied.

"I'm here to do a job, Reece, not get caught up in some tabloid news."

"I understand. I've been down that road with Cyrus. You need to be honest with yourself, Arianna," Reece advised.

"I will. Now, what colors do we want to do for the event?"

"I think black and white is fine, nothing over the top. We should let the people who bid on dinner pick the loca-tions," Reece stated.

I continued to take notes from Reece, and we ended

up ordering lunch after three hours of picking the drivers we'd want for the race. We heard a knock on the door, and I called out for them to enter.

"I have lunch from your favorite place, ladies," Tisha said, carrying in bags from Surf Shack.

"I can guess who sent this over," I replied.

Tisha placed the bags down on my desk, pulling out napkins and paper plates. I sipped on the sweet tea and grabbed a French fry, savoring the food.

"This is so heavenly," Reece told me, rubbing her stomach.

"Cyrus knows his woman," I bellowed out.

"Won't be much longer when someone scoops you up." Ree chuckled.

"My mind is telling me no."

"But if Kash came through that door right now, your body would say something different," Reece joked.

"He called me Ari when I was at Jackson's office," I said.

"Ohhh, he has special privileges then. You only let your brother or close friends call you that," Reece responded, taking a bite of her wrap.

"Reece, you're thinking too hard on this, friend."

"I get called friend when I call you out. Bestie when I agree with you!" Reece taunted.

I took another bite of my sandwich, ignoring her underhanded comment.

"Between you and Essence, I can't win, no matter what."

Tisha closed the door of my office after setting everything out.

"The best way to be a best friend is to keep you on your toes, babe," Reece replied.

"Just wait for when Essence gets with somebody; I can see her obsessing over every little thing," I mentioned.

"Essence would probably have us following the guy if he doesn't call her after a day or two of meeting," Reece joked.

I howled at her comment because Essence would be the type. We continued talking and planning the charity event for later in the month.

* * *

Later in the day, I pulled up to the salon to get my hair touched up. The braids were pulling apart too early, and I needed to be prepared for my race. Grabbing my keys and purse and stepping out of my car, I headed up to the door, pulled it back, and stepped inside. Scanning the room, I noticed my stylist was finishing up with someone in her chair. I waved to the owner and receptionist of Just Cutz by Justine. I'd been coming to her shop since I was sixteen years old. She was a longtime family friend and stylist of our family.

"Hey, Justine," I said.

"Hey, Arianna. How are you?" she replied.

"I'm good. How are you doing?"

"Working as usual, keeping these crazy girls in check," Justine announced loudly.

"Don't hurt them too much." I chortled and sat in Louise's chair, placing my purse on top of her stylist desk.

"What's going on with you?" Louise asked.

"Nothing," I responded.

"Arianna, I've seen your face plastered on all the blogs," Louise replied.

The door chimed, and a group of three girls walked

inside, laughing and whispering together. Louise placed a cape around me, grabbed my hair to rebraid as I pulled my phone out of my pocket to send a text.

"Oh my god! I can't wait to get my hair done for my date with Kash," some woman said, sitting in the chair next to Louise's booth.

"This party is going to be epic," her friend replied.

"Big Top is going to have it VIP tight. Make sure our names are on the list," the short red-haired girl said.

"Already taken care of, Brittney. I'm sleeping with the bartender," her friend said, slapping hands with the redhead.

"So, tell me about this boy who's a car racer?" Justine commented, and the three girls looked over at us.

"Nothing to tell, Justine," I answered, shifting in my seat.

"He's cute but looks like trouble. I mean his name is Kash, right?" Justine asked, watching Louise clip my ends.

"Excuse me, are you talking about Kamden Kash Coleman?" the redheaded girl named Brittney called out toward me.

"No," I told her.

She stood, walked over to me, and crossed her arms over her chest, tilting her head to the left. I narrowed my eyes, waiting for her to say something. Fighting over a guy I wasn't involved with was laughable.

"Good, because after this party, he's going to be mine."

"Uhm... I think you should get your friend. I think she's confused," I responded.

"Brittney, take a seat if you want me to do your hair. I suggest you go back to your seat," Justine demanded, pointing to the couch in the lobby.

"Sorry, Justine. I need to make sure my man isn't being taken advantage of with these groupies," Brittney said.

"Groupie!" I cackled in my seat.

"Brittney, take a seat, please. Arianna, hush and turn back around," Justine said as she pulled the cape from around me.

"Okay, you're all set, Arianna," Justine told me.

"Thanks, Justine. Don't forget the charity event is coming up this month. I'll have an invitation sent over," I said.

"Thanks, and try to not get in any more fights, please," Justine implored.

"I promise," I answered.

Amusement gleamed in my eyes as I walked past while they whispered to each other. I paid the receptionist and left the salon to head home for the day.

Chapter Six

Arianna

Flashback – Las Vegas

The loud bass of Drake played through the speakers as the women danced in front of him while security stood around the VIP section. Once work finished, I flew out to the Venetian to the grand opening of the club and had bottle service ready for me. My usual VIP suite was set up for me, Reece, and Essence, with Cîroc, champagne, vodka, and food. We had sliders and fries to consume up the alcohol I had ordered. Essence danced in her seat while she sipped on the champagne.

My favorite song came on as I stood to dance next to Essence. I glanced around the club and noticed the crowd getting hyped from the latest single from Meghan Thee Stallion. Out of the corner of my eye, a familiar person stepped up to the sanctioned rope of my section. He whispered to the security guard, and I continued playing it off, waiting to see what he did. He wore a black shirt with the first few buttons open, black pants, and a leather jacket. I turned to listen to Essence talking to me.

"What did you say?" I asked.

"*Is that who I think it is?*" *Essence motioned to Kash.*

I smiled, winking at her while looking over my shoulder at Reece hugging Kash and laughing. I knew with him being a driver for Cyrus, she knew him. With me at the office part time, I never saw him up close unless an event was happening.

"*Yeah.*"

"*Arianna, I want you to meet someone,*" *Reece called out.*

Angling toward them, I smiled and held my hand out for him to shake. Much to my surprise, he pulled me up against him, staring into my eyes.

"*Someone's a little overzealous,*" *I spoke, peering up at the smile on his face. He bit his bottom lip, wrapping his hand around my waist.*

"*I go after what I want,*" *Kash commented.*

"*What is it that you want?*" *I questioned, stepping out of his hold.*

"*You.*"

"*Too bad, your girlfriends don't think it's a good idea.*"

"*I'm a single man, sweetheart.*"

I grinned and asked, "Single, huh?"

"*Very much so,*" *Kash said before he gripped my palm, holding it up to his lips for a kiss.*

"*I like your style.*"

"*I can say the same to you. How about you hang with my team, or we can be alone to celebrate my win?*" *Kash asked, the fixed intensity of his laser stare giving me shivers. I looked over his shoulder at the groupies making out with his friends and decided to take matters into my own hands.*

"*How about we make it a duo evening?*"

His eyebrow arched in surprise.

"Seriously."

"Yes. I want to see what Kash is all about."

"Baby, you don't want to know what I'm all about. You might not like what you see," Kash told me, running a hand up my back, pressing me into his chest.

"Maybe I can surprise you. Let's go to your room."

"What about your friends?" Kash asked.

"They'll be fine. Let me tell them I'm leaving with you."

"So, you're just going to take off like that? What about a boyfriend?"

"I don't have a boyfriend."

"I wouldn't care if you did anyway," Kash stated.

I held up a finger and stepped out of his hold to tell Reece and Essence I was leaving.

I picked up my clutch and kissed Essence on the cheek.

"I'll see you later. I'm heading out with Kash," I announced.

"Wait, how well do you know him?" Essence remarked.

"He's a race car driver for Cyrus. I know him, and he's cute. Momma needs to have a little fun."

"Kash is a playboy and arrogant, Arianna. More than likely, he won't call you tomorrow," Reece stated. Bending down, I hugged and whispered in her ear.

"That's the plan," I said.

"When will I find a sexy, rich, rude boy?" Essence commented.

"Keep looking around; there's a club full of people," I said, waving before I grabbed Kash's hand. Moving through the crowd toward the VIP exit, the photographers were hanging out and took a few shots of us as I tried to hide my face.

Kash hit the elevator for the penthouse and pulled me in front of him. His breath against my ear caused a tingling up my spine, as his arousal pressed against my leg.

"Going up," Kash said, peering from my lips to my eyes for confirmation of what we were about to do. I met him halfway, capturing his lips. The elevator dinged, and he groaned, breaking away to pull me into the elevator as security stood downstairs on watch. This was the VIP elevator they gave out to members of high profile who stayed at the hotel. I hated having to stop from the pleasurable sensations of our tongues as they meshed together. He pushed me up against the elevator, brushing his hand across my cheek.

"Are you sure about this, Arianna?" Kash asked.

"Yes," I said, feeling the heat of a blush on my cheeks.

"Good."

The elevator dinged, and he backed up. He grasped my hand, and I bit my bottom lip, giggling at him smacking me on the ass.

"Damn," Kash said.

"What are you celebrating tonight?"

"Let's not talk about work tonight."

"Keep it mysterious... huh."

"One night is all I can give you, baby."

"Why do you keep calling me baby? I'm not your girlfriend."

"It's a habit," he said, opening the door of the room, and I walked inside.

"Nice penthouse," I said, looking around. It was set up like the suite we had on either end of the hotel. Large, sunken living room, kitchen connected to the living room with a huge flat screen hanging from the ceiling, and large windows decorated in gold and cream colors. I stepped up to the window and watched over the city when I felt his presence behind me. His hands started below, slowly skimming from the bottom of my dress. I wore a short cocktail dress that could be pulled over my head. Kash's hand slid up my stomach, as he pressed his groin behind me. My hand went flat on the window.

"Kashhh..." I groaned.

"You're beautiful as fuck."

"I bet you tell every woman that."

He chuckled behind me, pulled my hair behind my ear, lingering a trail of kisses.

"I promise you're the first one I'm thinking of doing many naughty things to without wanting anything in return," he said, his breath tickling my ear.

"Mhmmm..." I moaned as his hand pulled both sides of my thong.

"Your voice sounds so sweet. How old are you?" Kash asked me.

"Old enough. I'm twenty-three, and you?" I asked as I turned around, helping him remove his jacket.

"Twenty-five," he said, clasping me to him and lifting me up. I wrapped my legs around his waist.

Our lips crashed into each other, and his tongue gave a teasing lap with my own. I ran a palm over his hair.

"Mmmmm..." he grunted, walking us back to his bedroom. I planted my feet down, removing my dress as he unbuckled his pants before rubbing up his muscular chest. His deep-brown eyes oozed a longing to want more than what the night was meant to be. If I were in another headspace, I could see something happening with Kash as a boyfriend. But the playboy I read about in all the gossip blogs was never a one-woman type of man.

"Lay on your back with your legs open," Kash said.

I kept eye contact and walked backwards to the king-size bed and slid back. It was plush with cream and gold comforters. The rest of the room held a loveseat, small bar, and a vanity mirror with two large, horizontal windows. Kash crawled up the bed, taking his wallet out of his pocket and removing the condom. He tossed it on the bed as he laid flat on the bed, facing my sex.

"No turning back, Arianna."

"I should say the same to you."

He grinned, winked, and dove his tongue into my sex, causing me to arch off the bed at the moment of contact.

"Kash!" I moaned.

"Ahhhh..." Kash moaned.

"Fuck! Right there, touch me," I purred.

"Tell me you like this?" Kash questioned.

Squirming in his arms, I couldn't help it when my legs locked him in place, and one of my arms gripped his head as I braced for another shock of pleasure as his tongue swiped across my lips.

"Ughh... Kash," I cried out, feeling his finger slide over my bud.

"Shit, you taste just like I thought," Kash remarked, torching me with double penetration of his tongue and thumb.

"Please... K.k.k, I'm coming!" I screamed, feeling the sheets soaked with my juices.

"Come for me, sweetheart."

"Ahhhh! Yessss," I said, feeling the room spin from the powerful orgasm. I tried to grab the pillow to put between my legs, and Kash chuckled, removing it as he picked the condom up and removed his pants and shoes.

"No time for sleeping, baby. I got you for the rest of the night, and I plan to keep you satisfied with my dick and

tongue," Kash told me, lying behind me and lifting my leg as he eased his dick into my pussy. I grasped the sheet as his pace picked up.

"Fuck! You feel so good," Kash grunted.

I took in a deep breath, feeling him in my stomach as I laid my head back against his chest.

"Ohhh... Kash... Shittt!"

I felt his hand on my clit.

"Arianna... Ughh... Damn. I need you on your knees," Kash said, smacking my ass as he adjusted me flat on my stomach. He entwined our hands, spread them out wide, and hovered over my back. Feeling his hot, alcohol-infused breath sent a tingling up my spine.

"Oh my god! You're too big."

Kash bent down, sucking on my neck, rolling his hips.

"Let it out, gorgeous," Kash coached.

"Kash! I'm coming again," I screamed from the intense pressure.

"Me too, sweetheart. Fuck! Come for me."

I did, and he tightened his hold, falling on my back, pumping slowly, and breathing hard in my ear. After a few seconds, he rolled over, out of breath.

"I need to get cleaned up," I said. Kash pulled me on top of him, kissed and bit my bottom lip.

"I'm not ready for you to go. Let's order some food, and you can show me your riding skills."

"I have to warn you. Men tend to fall in love with me after I put them to sleep," I jested.

He smirked. "I'm not most men, baby," he answered by pulling out another condom, and I smashed my lips to him. We continued having sex in every corner of his room and living room until we passed out.

Present Day

I woke up from my dream by the ringing of the doorbell. Cicely was off, so I got up, wrapping my robe around me. Closing my bedroom door, I heard banging alongside the doorbell ringing again.

"What do you want?" I snapped as I opened the door and saw who it was.

Freddie stood smiling at me as though I should be happy to see him.

"I missed you, baby," Freddie said.

"Okay, and?"

"Can we talk, please? We owe it to ourselves to get some things clear," Freddie explained as he stepped inside without me inviting him.

"Fine, explain yourself, but nothing is going to change," I told him.

"You don't mean that, Arianna." Freddie reached out to grab my hand, and I yanked it away, before walking over and sitting down on my couch.

"Freddie, say what needs to be said and please leave afterwards," I replied.

He sat next to me, and I leaned over to grab the remote.

"How are you?" Freddie questioned.

"Fine. Now, get to the reason why you needed to bang on my door at ten at night."

"I want a second chance, Arianna. I was stupid, selfish, and it took me hitting rock bottom to realize you were the best thing to ever happen to me."

"Thank you for realizing that, Freddie, but I'm not interested in going backwards," I answered.

"Wait, are you seeing someone?" Freddie asked.

"No, but it doesn't matter. My life is complicated right now."

He ran a hand down his face, sighed, and stood.

"I'll give you some time, Arianna. I'm not giving up," Freddie said.

"Don't waste your time, Freddie," I said, thinking about the encounter at the office, but I felt something stirring in my heart that I didn't like. He tried to lean down to kiss me on the lips, only I shifted my face, and his lips landed on my cheek. I watched him walk out of the house then I stood, walking to the kitchen to get a glass of wine to help me sleep. Dating Freddie again wasn't happening, so I hoped he would find someone who was looking for what he wanted.

Chapter Seven

Kamden

Two weeks later

I bumped knuckles with Tripp and Brody, my pit crew, as the first race of the official season started. I had Ralph behind me, setting everything up. He was another driver on the team that was a friend of mine.

"Are you ready for this?" Cyrus questioned.

"Most definitely. Are you out there today?"

"I have work to do in the office, so you have a fair chance today," Cyrus jested.

"You let Reece gas up your head."

I heard the roaring of the car and looked back at Ralph's face scrunched up in worry. I shook it off, not paying attention.

"How's he doing?" Cyrus asked as he motioned to Ralph.

He was pissed that my timeout from racing from the Vegas trip was over, and I could start today. I'd known Ralph for a few years and considered him a friend, but lately, he'd been distant. I wasn't sure if it was because his career wasn't where he wanted it to be or because he was just jealous of me.

"Not sure; he's been on and off lately. It doesn't help that his numbers aren't good," I answered.

"I see the jealousy in his eyes. Be careful with him," Cyrus said.

"I will."

"What's up with you and Arianna?"

"Nothing," I said, stepping out of the car and grabbing my helmet.

"She works for Cyrus Premier Enterprises and is Reece's best friend. Don't screw her over," Cyrus stated.

"Coming from you, that must mean something," I chortled.

"Ha-Ha... It only takes one fuck up, and she's gone. I like Arianna and don't want her to get hurt because you can't keep it in your pants," Cyrus said, tapping my helmet.

"Where's Brody?" I asked, changing the subject.

"The old change of conversation doesn't work with me. Listen, she's racing and planning the charity event. Keep it civil," Cyrus said.

"Why again is she racing?" I questioned.

"Because I've been training her, and she has the passion to be out on the track like you and me. Are you scared?" Cyrus replied.

"She's a girl. I have nothing to be scared of."

"She might surprise you," Cyrus implied, walking off toward his office.

Tripp came up next to the car to help me push it out.

"Ready to go?" Tripp asked.

"Ready, my boy."

The cars lined up, and the pit crews moved away as

I slid inside. I heard Brody come in on the radio to direct me as the timer started. Revving up the engine as the crowd cheered on, this was where I felt the excitement, rush, and fire to be on top. I pulled off as the team clapped and yelled in excitement. Keeping a steady pace, I was ahead of the other drivers by a split second.

"Control it, Kash. Keep it lined up, you're doing fine," Brody said.

"On it, Brody."

Two hours later, the race was over, I showered, cleaned up, and met Tripp and Ralph for lunch to celebrate at Surf Shack. Cyrus told me about this place, and I'd been meaning to come here. Finally relaxing after the run and the week of craziness, I was back to chilling.

"Good job, Kash. You're back in the top spot," Tripp said.

"Thanks, it's good to be back on the track," I replied.

"What's up with you and Josie?" Ralph questioned, out of the blue.

"Nothing. If you ask my mom, she'd say I was crazy for even dealing with her."

"She's right." Tripp coughed in laughter, taking a sip of his water.

"She's not that bad," I replied.

"So, you two aren't a couple?" Ralph investigated.

I stopped picking up the fork and peered over at him in curiosity.

"Ask me what you really want to ask me?"

"She told me that you cheated on her, and I didn't know if you two were serious. Looking out for you," Ralph explained.

"Wait, you want to date Josie?" I asked.

"I don't go after your dates, Kash. I think I can manage getting my own women," Ralph insisted.

Tripp and I both stared at each other after that comment. We had a healthy competition amongst the drivers, but sometimes Ralph had taken this a little farther and ended up in fights.

"What are your plans after this?" Tripp asked, eating his sub sandwich.

"My mom called and wants me to come over to put some things up in the garage," I responded.

"I'll head over with you," Tripp stated.

"Cool. What about you, Ralph?"

"I got a date," Ralph told us, grinning and rubbing his hands together.

"Does she have a pulse?" Tripp joked.

Ralph flipped him off and talked about some new chick he was interested in getting with. I zoned him out when a group of women came to my table to ask for an autograph.

"Oh my god! It's really you. Can I take a picture, please?" A young girl no older than seventeen or eighteen asked.

"Of course. What's your name?" I questioned.

"Kelsey," she said.

I extended a hand toward her, and she screamed, causing the entire restaurant to look at us.

* * *

An hour and a half later, Tripp sat in the passenger seat. I had the music up, bumping to the latest track from Kendrick Lamar. Tripp tried to turn it down, and I slapped his hand away.

"You know I don't let anybody fool with my music."

"Are you going to that party this weekend?" Tripp asked.

"Yeah, Sarai has me as the VIP guest. I'm getting paid to appear," I replied.

"Cool. I might swing through. But what's up with your boy, Big Ra?" He used his nickname that only came out when someone had something negative to say about Ralph.

"As far as I know, nothing. Why?"

"I don't know yet. He just seems off, like he's hiding something." I drove down Pacific Highway to my mom's place. She lived in the same neighborhood that Cyrus lived after he mentioned the peacefulness he had from the paparazzi. I'd thought about moving in the same area, but I liked being near the city of L.A. in my condo. Turning into my mom's driveway, I turned the car off.

"He's always been to himself." I opened the driver's door, slamming it shut, and saw the front door swing open. My mom stood with her hands on her hips and a towel in her hand.

"Why am I hearing about you getting engaged and having a baby?" Mom asked. I raised my arms to give her a hug, and she pushed me back.

"Ma, you know how the media takes things and runs with them."

"I don't know what the media does because my son is always into some type of drama," Mom told me.

"Ma, you remember Tripp," I said, planting a kiss on her forehead.

"Tripp, do you worry your mother the way Kash worries me?" she asked, turning her back to head inside the house.

He exchanged a smile with her, then shook his head. "No, ma'am," Tripp said.

"He's lying, Ma," I said. I shoved him in the arm, and he play boxed with me.

"Anyone hungry?" Mom asked as she sauntered off to the kitchen.

I rubbed my stomach "No, we just ate."

"Tell me about this woman, Kamden," she demanded.

I groaned, not in the mood to have another conversation about my love life.

"The only woman I'm worried about is you," I replied.

"Josie called me," Mom said as she pulled the cookies out of the oven.

Josie was a longtime friend who I happened to have sex with every blue moon. Nothing serious between us on my end, but over time, her feelings had changed, and I told her I wasn't looking for anything serious. I wasn't the commitment type. She worked as a sports reporter, and our schedules worked out to benefit us both. Now to hear that she'd reached out to my mom to get in good wouldn't fly with me.

"What did she say?"

"She wanted to know why you're ignoring her calls. I never liked her for you; she seemed like an opportunist," Mom explained.

Something we both agreed about. Josie could manipulate any situation and often, if I didn't call her back, she'd show up at the racetrack or my house trying to get me to talk with her.

"I'll take care of it, Ma. Don't worry."

"This new girl though, she's pretty," Ma stated, passing the plate of cookies to me. She opened the fridge next to the oven and grabbed the milk and glasses.

The image of her melted away like mist before the sun. "Ma," I said.

She gave Tripp a subtle wink, giving him a glass and pouring milk inside.

"Have you met her, Tripp?" Mom asked.

"No, I know of her though. She's related to the Pierce family," Tripp said.

"Ohhh," Mom said.

"Yep, a billion-dollar family," Tripp said.

My voice was laced with irritation. "I don't care about her money."

"We know, honey. I didn't raise you to look at someone based on looks or financial gain," Mom told me.

"What do you need to put up in the garage?" I tugged at my collar, wrapping an arm around her shoulder.

"A few boxes in the corner need to go up."

"Have you talked with Reece and Cyrus?" I questioned. They often checked up on her for me to keep me updated. She didn't care for it, but since she was retired, and I traveled so much, it kept my mind at ease. Well, more like I told her to quit working so I could spoil her, send her on trips around the world.

"I saw them yesterday," she said, opening the garage door. I looked around and noticed a stack of boxes that needed to be organized.

"She works with Cyrus."

"Who?" she asked.

"The girl from Vegas," I said before I bent down and blew the dust off the top. I saw boxes of my stuff from when I was a baby.

"You like her?"

"She's interesting, but I'm not looking for anything serious," I responded and picked the large box up and stacked it on top of the shelf.

"Tripp, grab that box over there, please," Mom stated.

He nodded and tossed the entire cookie in his mouth and grabbed the box off the floor.

I stayed at her place until late, helping to clean up. I then dropped Tripp off at home around midnight. When I pulled up, I saw a car in my guest spot. I lived in a gated community and somehow, Josie was able to get inside, which meant she used her credentials. I turned the car off and stepped out when she climbed out of hers.

"Kash, let me explain," Josie rushed out.

My jaw clenched at her intrusion, and I yanked out of her hold.

"Josie, we have nothing to talk about. We haven't slept together in over nine months."

"I miss you," Josie said, following behind me to my building.

Typing in my code, I walked inside, and she followed.

"You can't be here, Josie."

"Why? Is there another woman here?"

Checking with the receptionist at the lobby, I grabbed my mail and headed to the elevator with Josie on my tail. I typed in the code to the elevator and stepped on when it dinged. Josie tried to step on, and I stopped her.

"If I do, it's none of your business."

"Is it that bitch from Vegas?"

"You realize I never made you believe I wanted a relationship, right?" I questioned.

"Kash, wait!" Josie yelled out as the doors closed.

I rubbed the back of my head to get the tension out of my neck. A few seconds later, the door opened, and I walked out and bumped into a soft body. I captured her around the waist before she fell.

It was either her perfume or body wash, but it caused me to grip her hips even tighter in jealousy.

"What are you doing here so late?" I questioned.

"Kash, what are you doing here?" Arianna spoke.

"I live here," I said.

"Oh. Ummm... can you let me go?" she asked.

"What if I don't want to?" I said, running a hand up her back.

"I would have to call my brother to kick your ass," she stated, and I wanted to challenge her further.

"Your brother lives here?"

"Malik does. What about you?" Arianna asked.

"Same. I didn't know I had a Pierce living in my building," I said, releasing her and taking my keys out to open the door.

"Have a good night," Arianna responded as she attempted to leave when I called her name.

"Why not come in for a drink?"

"I don't think that's a good idea. We've caused enough drama for the blogs," Arianna stated as she tapped on the elevator button.

"Come on, one drink and a little conversation. I won't bite. I promise," I insisted, opening the door wider. She looked toward her brother's door in thought, then gazed at the elevator, and finally her eyes settled on me. A second went by, and she let the elevator doors close, opting to walk into my condo.

Chapter Eight

Kamden

"How was your day?" I asked as I dropped my keys on top of my desk. I recently had a decorator come over and redo everything for a magazine spread on sports athletes' celebrity homes. She styled it with a Southern laid-back feel. Not too masculine for a bachelor pad, but a family vibe with a large fireplace, windows that opened automatically with draped curtains, and gray and black colors throughout. I had three bedrooms and two baths. The condo had a gym as well as a pool with a theater if anyone threw parties. I mostly kept to myself and never interacted with any neighbors.

Arianna laughed at my question.

"Why is that funny?" I questioned as I opened the cabinet and grabbed two wine glasses. I then turned toward the walk-in pantry to pulled a bottle of wine out.

"You don't seem like the type to ask someone how their day is."

Meeting her at the couch, I passed the red wine over to her and took a seat.

"I can surprise you," I replied.

"Except when it comes to me racing, right?" she asked.

"When did you want to get into racing? I mean, your family seems very well off."

"That's my family, not me. I work for everything I have, Kash."

I held a hand up, interrupting her.

"Call me Kamden," I said.

"I like Kash."

"I want you to call me Kamden."

"Why?"

"Because the people I'm close to, and I consider special, call me Kamden."

"You just met me only a few weeks ago!"

"I know, and it's crazy that I can't get you out of my head. Even though I keep saying it didn't mean anything."

"Me too," Arianna remarked.

"How many siblings do you have?"

"Two brothers. I'm the baby of the family, and Malik is the middle child," Arianna said, taking a sip of her wine and crossing her legs. I finally noticed she was wearing a simple pair of jeans, a white t-shirt, and minimal makeup. But she looked more beautiful than she did in Vegas.

"I like this look on you," I said aloud.

"People think I never dress down, but I had to go to the track for practice and wanted to be comfortable."

"Are you serious about racing this week?"

"Yep. So, don't get scared now and back out."

"I have an idea," I said.

"What is your idea, Kamden?" She softly asked, leaning back on my couch, tossing her arm on the back. I noticed her pink bra underneath that fell off her arm as she got more comfortable. I recalled tasting her sweet nipples as they hardened at my touch.

"I like hearing you call me Kamden."

"Don't get too comfortable with it."

"If you win the race, I'll donate to the charity with a blank check, and you pick the amount."

"You can't be serious."

"I am."

"What do you get if you win?" Arianna asked.

"A date with you."

"We already had sex," Arianna recalled, shifting in her seat.

"And it caused international news, I remember. But I'd like an official date if I win."

"Just a date and nothing else, right?" Arianna inquired.

"A date with you, and if you win, I'll let you name the price of the check for the charity ride."

"It seems like I'm coming out the winner on this bet. I mean, what if I say one million for charity?" she gauged for an answer.

I shrugged and refilled my wine.

"Then, it's a million."

She gulped the rest of her wine before she nudged it over for me to refill.

"What if I say five million?" she queried with a furrowed brow.

"I have no limit, Arianna. Give me your price if you win, but I don't plan on losing though."

"Any brothers and sisters?" Arianna questioned.

"Nope, only child of my mother. Dad left me when I was younger."

"When did you get into racing?" Arianna asked.

"When I was younger, the same story. Kid pissed off from his dad walking out, and he gets in with the wrong crowd and goes off doing things that could lead him to jail. Mom signed me up to be a mentor at The All Hands Home where Reece worked when I was younger and through Cyrus Premier Enterprises, I met Cyrus, and we became friends," I explained.

"Now you're this big star."

"Something like that."

"What about your girlfriend?" she asked, sipping slowly. My dick swelled when her lips opened and enclosed around the rim of the glass.

I cleared my throat, thinking of something else to keep him from being noticed. I thought of rainbows and cows.

"No girlfriend. I do have a few women I hang out with from time to time," I answered.

"Hangout as in a sexual relationship?" she inquired.

"Mutually agreed upon sexual experiences," I answered.

"A fuck buddy? It's okay, Kamden. I do the same thing."

I glowered at her statement.

"When was the last time you'd been with someone besides me?"

"Not that I need to tell you this. But you were the only person I was with since my breakup, six or seven months ago."

"Why did you break up?"

"You ask a lot of questions," she said, checking her watch.

"You need to go?"

"Yeah, it's getting late. I need to get some rest before

work, and I have practice tomorrow," Arianna said, standing.

I placed my glass down and followed behind her.

"Let me walk you to your car," I said.

"You don't need to do that," Arianna said.

"I might be an ass sometimes, but my mother did teach me manners. Let me walk you down to your car at least."

"Fine, and it's a bet," Arianna replied as she stuck her hand out for me to shake on it.

I gently pulled it up to my lips and kissed each finger as she gasped in response.

"No backing out of this bet," I told her.

"Don't get too cocky, Mr. Coleman," Arianna said, patting my chest. I held the door open for her, and she stepped out as I locked it behind me. I followed her into the elevator as the doors opened. We continued talking about her job at Cyrus Premier Enterprises and the charity work she was involved in at Pierce Motors. After leaving the building, I opened the driver's side door to her car as she slid inside and started it up. The window rolled down, and I leaned down to say good night.

"Nice talking with you, Arianna. Don't forget our bet. Make sure you wear something red. It's my favorite color," I said.

She laughed and shook her head.

"Very presumptuous, don't you think?" Arianna retorted.

"Not at all, baby." I kissed her cheek and stood back as she turned the lights on and sped out of the parking structure in her Audi.

"Damn, she's going to be a handful," I said aloud and walked back into my building to sleep for the day.

* * *

The next morning, I was up eating breakfast that my housekeeper made for me. I'd recently hired someone to help out around when I was away, and she came highly recommended through Reece. I felt someone staring at me and looked up to catch Cicely eyeing me suspiciously.

"What?"

"Kash, you need to be more responsible," Cicely said.

"What happened to Mr. Coleman?" I teased. I liked getting under her skin. She reminded me of a second mom. She'd been with me for two months now, and I often heard about how I was living the playboy life that would end with me alone and heartbroken if I didn't commit to someone.

"That lasted one day, until I could figure you out," Cicely teased, and I burst out in laughter.

"I thought it was my job to research and figure you out. How did I end up at the wrong party?"

"Because you run around and do God knows what with these girls. I have to hear about it from your mom and see it in these tabloids," Cicely mentioned.

"You can't believe everything in the paper, Cicely."

"Oh, I know. But your latest situation is close to home."

"What do you mean?"

"I know the Pierce family very well and if you hurt my baby—" I raised my hand, cutting her off.

"Woman, tell me who you're talking about before you threaten me. So dramatic at times, Cicely," I said aloud even though I meant to think it in my head. Now, she had a harsh glare across her face.

"Sorry, Cicely."

"You know better," Cicely said, wiping the counter down and putting the leftover juice in the fridge.

"Are you talking about Arianna?"

"Yes, and I know she can be tough at times and comes across like she has everything together. She's the baby of the family and spoiled."

"Oh, I know," I answered.

"Which means you and your womanizing ways need to stay away if you aren't going to do right by her."

"Who said anything about me hurting her?"

"I see the type of guys she gets involved with, and you're different. I can see her falling for you, and you've never been in love from what I hear from your mom. Except that damn Josie constantly popping up."

"Josie's a friend," I said.

"A friend who has expectations of being more," Cicely stated, removing my plate and tossing the leftovers away.

"Remind me to never tell my mom anything."

"Stop being a brat and be honest with yourself, Kamden. You're twenty-five and living your bachelor life. Nothing's wrong with that but remember to be careful with the women you date," Cicely said. I agreed, giving a thumb's up.

"Thanks, Cicely." I stood, kissing her cheek, taking a final sip of the orange juice, and placing the glass in the sink.

She waved me off with the towel, and I headed to get dressed for the day. Sliding on my jeans, I grabbed my phone and saw a few messages from Josie.

Josie: *Kash, call me, please.*

Me: *What's up, Josie?*

Josie: *I need to talk to you...*

Me: *About what?*

Josie: *Can we meet in person?*

Me: *I need to get to practice!*

Josie: *I can come to you.*

Me: *Fine, but this better be important.*

Josie: *Maybe we can do lunch or dinner?*

Me: *No, I only agreed to talk.*

Josie: *Okay, I'll see you soon.*

"Women," I said then grabbed a t-shirt and jacket, picking up my motorcycle helmet and keys.

"Be safe, Kash," Cicely yelled from the kitchen.

"Always, CiCi!"

I shut the door, headed toward the elevator, and hit the button. A few seconds later, the door was stopped by a hand, and I looked up, noticing it was Malik Pierce.

"Kash," Malik said.

"Malik."

He stood off to the left side of the elevator, and I leaned on the right when the doors closed, and silence resonated in the closed space.

"Stay away from my sister," Malik muttered.

"I'm sorry?"

"Ari, stay away from her," Malik said when the elevator stopped in the lobby.

"She's an adult, Malik." He stepped off first and turned toward me at my last comment.

"That's my little sister. She may appear hard on the outside, but she can be a little spontaneous and overzealous with her heart," Malik stated.

"Listen, if something does happen, it's between me and Ari. I'm not saying anything has happened beyond the Vegas thing." He cringed at my remark.

"Which should tell you it's not something you should continue investing your time into," Malik answered.

I closed the space between us, making eye contact so he knew I wasn't some little kid.

"Arianna can make her own decisions. You know her better than me. She doesn't talk to people trying to tell her what to do," I said and walked around him and out the door.

* * *

Forty minutes later, I was at the track. I parked my bike, took my helmet off, and stepped through the office, speaking to the staff and crew. I then headed to the garage for some laps before the official charity event.

"I didn't know you'd be here today," Tripp said.

"Yeah, I need to get a few laps in before the charity event. Is Cyrus here?" I asked.

"Yeah, with Reece in his office," Tripp replied.

"Perfect," I said and went to talk with them.

Before I could get too far, Josie called out my name.

"Kash!" Josie rushed out and stalked toward me.

"Josie."

"I missed you," she said and attempted to kiss me on the lips again right as a flash went off.

I pushed her behind me and tried to grab the camera from the photographer.

"What the fuck?" I screamed.

"Kash, calm down."

"Calm down, how the hell did they get in here?" I questioned as I grabbed his camera to take the film out, but I couldn't figure it out, so I dropped it on the ground.

"Hey, man! That's my camera," the photographer shouted.

"This is private property," I replied.

"Kash, it's just a photo," Josie said. I looked over at her and shook my head.

"Did you set this up?" I yelled.

"What? No, of course not!"

"Mighty funny, the second you text me to talk, a photographer shows up, Josie."

"You're acting crazy, Kash," Josie remarked.

"You owe me for that camera, dude," the photographer stated.

"Fuck your camera, man, and get out of here before I kick your ass," I shouted.

"Are you serious right now?" Josie questioned, stepping between me and the photographer.

"Very serious and since you set me up, you can get out with him," I told her and walked off and heard her heels behind me.

"Kash! Kash! Wait, please," Josie said.

"I'm putting this on all the blogs. Wait until I sue your ass!" The photographer yelled.

Josie grasped my arm and turned me to face her.

"Kash, listen, I didn't have anything to do with him taking our photo," Josie pleaded.

I ran a hand through my hair. "It doesn't matter, Josie. It looks off and lets me know I can't trust you." I heard laughter behind me, and Josie's face grimaced.

"Hey, Kash," Reece spoke while Cyrus stood there holding her hand.

"Hey, Reece. What's up, Cyrus?" I asked.

"Is everything okay?" Reece asked, looking between Josie and me.

Chapter Nine

Kamden

"Uhm... yeah. You remember Josie from Sports Channel Six?" I spoke.

"Hi, Josie," Reece said, extending her hand to Josie.

Josie looked at her hand for a second before shaking it. I thought it was strange, but I wouldn't get into it right now.

"Hi," Josie replied.

"Okay. Well, we need to get going, Cyrus," Reece said.

"Where are you two going?" I asked.

"To talk with Arianna about the charity event," Cyrus stated.

"I'll tag along," I said.

"What! No, we're supposed to do lunch," Josie said.

"I didn't know you two were dating, Kash," Reece said.

"We're not."

"Not yet," Josie implied, rubbing up against my cheek.

I moved her hand away gently and continued talking to Cyrus.

"Did Arianna tell you about the bet?" I questioned.

"No, what bet?" Reece asked.

"If she wins the race, I donate any amount she wants to the charity. If I win, she has to go on a date with me."

"Kash!" Josie screamed.

"Josie! What are you doing here?" I heard and then saw Ralph walking toward us.

"Talking with Kash," Josie answered.

"Can I talk to you?" Ralph asked Josie.

I raised an eyebrow in surprise.

"No, I'm here with my boyfriend," Josie commented.

"Boyfriend!" Ralph and I yelled at the same time in disbelief.

"This is like some soap opera," Cyrus mumbled.

"Kash, stop acting like we don't mean anything to each other," Josie muttered as she stood on her tippy toes to try to kiss me again, only I jerked back. Don't get me wrong, Josie was a beautiful woman, did a great job, was smart, funny, and graduated with a degree in sports analysis. She was five-seven and looked like she could be a model if she wanted. She had a rosy undertone with a sandy complexion from her constantly tanning, along with pouty lips, green eyes, and high cheekbones. I could never take her seriously; she always wanted to be seen as my woman and not her own individual self.

"We don't, Josie. Ralph obviously is interested, so have fun," I responded and headed off to the pit to get suited up.

"Kash, hold up," Ralph said.

I groaned, not interested in what he had to say.

"Yeah, man," I said as I crossed my arms over my chest.

"Listen, I wasn't honest with you the other day at lunch," Ralph said.

"About?"

"Josie and me," Ralph said.

My ears picked up at that mention.

"You and Josie, huh?"

He looked over at Josie talking on her phone, staring at us.

"She came on to me one night," Ralph started to say, and I stopped him before he could give me all the sordid details.

"Listen, whatever you have going on with Josie, keep it to yourself. I don't need to know."

"I just want to make sure we're cool. I mean we race on the same team, and we're friends," Ralph said, and I saw a hint of cockiness cross his face.

Done being nice with everyone trying to play me for a fool, I punched him in the face.

"Kash!" Cyrus yelled and ran toward us. I grasped Ralph's jacket as security came over to break it up when Ralph tried to hit me back.

"Baby!" Josie yelled, running over to check if I was all right.

I yanked out of her grip.

"Get off me!" I said.

"Kash, you're done for the day. Go cool off," Cyrus said.

"This is some bullshit, Cyrus, and you know it," I said and snatched my keys out of my pocket and picked up my helmet to leave.

"Kamden, wait," Reece said.

I kicked the bike stand and sat, putting my helmet on.

"Reece, not now."

"What was that back there?" Reece asked.

"Nothing."

"It didn't look like nothing. Are you pissed that he's dating Josie, or that you actually like Arianna?" Reece questioned.

"Did Cyrus ever tell you that you think too hard about things?"

"Only when I'm right," Reece retorted, and we both chuckled.

"You're wrong this time, Reece. I like having my freedom."

"I see the spark in your eyes when I mention her name. Nothing's wrong with love, Kash," Reece stated, tapping the top of my helmet. I revved up the bike and rode off, heading to the house to see the boys for a little bit.

* * *

Flashback

I woke up groggy from the night before with a piece of paper on my face. I picked it up and read the note "Thanks" from the woman who disappeared and left me in bed alone. I chuckled, sitting up in bed and stretching. I checked the time on the clock and saw eight a.m. and moved the covers off me. Planting my feet on the warm carpet, I stood and walked to the restroom to piss. Washing my hands and brushing my teeth, I heard my phone ringing before I could turn the shower on. I strolled to the bedroom looking around and noticed it was coming from the living room.

Sarai's name flashed across the screen.

"Sarai, how's it going, beautiful?" I asked, getting under her skin as usual.

"You tell me, Kash. This morning, after finishing my normal routine, I went through my emails and guess what I saw?"

"What happened?"

"You on the cover of Diamond Gossip magazine going into a hotel room with a woman."

"Okay."

"Okay? Is that it?"

"I mean, yeah?"

"You should not be in Vegas, first of all. Second, you and your women are constantly in the media for the wrong reasons."

"Sarai, you worry too much," I said.

"That's my job, and now I have to try to put out statements that you're not engaged and having a baby."

"That's what I pay you for, right?"

"Don't get smart with me. How many times have I quit on you?"

I grunted, running a hand down my face, knowing she'd be quick to drop me in a split second. Hell, she'd done it more than two times. Sarai's a well-known publicist in the business. People get on waiting lists to have her represent them.

"I'm sorry, Sarai. How about I buy you a new Gucci belt?"

"Make it a belt and purse, and I might think about not dropping you," she said and hung up.

I looked at the phone and chuckled.

Ring! I heard the doorbell and grabbed the robe nearest to me and answered.

"Hello, sir! I came to clean, but I can come back later, if you want," the housekeeper said.

"No, you're good. Come inside," I replied and stepped back.

"I saw the young lady put the 'Do Not Disturb' on the door and wanted to make sure before entering," she said.

"Did she say anything when she left?" I questioned.

"No, she was talking on the phone at the time," she answered.

"Thanks. I'll be out of your way in a few minutes."

"No problem, take your time."

Present Day

I woke up from the dream of the morning after my night with Arianna. I heard screaming and yelling from the boys cheering each other on at the game. I was playing video games with them for a little while and must have fallen asleep after eating the pizza.

"Kash, when can we come to the track with you?" Shane asked.

I ruffled his hair and stretched.

"Ask Reece to set it up, and you can come whenever you're done with school. You know that's the most important thing," I said.

He nodded and ate another slice of pizza. Jumping up, I grabbed my jacket and helmet to head out when the door opened, and Reece walked in with Arianna.

"Speak of the devil," Reece said.

"Who, me?" I asked, pointing at myself.

"When did you get here?" Reece questioned.

"After I left the track. Arianna," I said.

"Hi, Kamden," Arianna replied.

"Did you order pizza for the boys?" Reece asked.

"Yeah, Jackson said it was okay. I ordered enough boxes if you're hungry," I replied, still staring at Arianna.

Reece looked from Arianna to me and shook her head.

"Shane, come help me grab the groceries out of the car," Reece stated, leaving me and Arianna alone.

"How was practice today?" I asked.

"Good," Arianna replied.

"Cool, you're ready to get your ass spanked?" I joked.

"I only like it spanked in the bedroom," Arianna teased, winking at me, and walking out of the house. I followed behind, not liking her answer.

"Where are you going?" I asked.

I waited for Reece and Shane to walk inside the house. I finally noticed what she was wearing—tight black leather pants, a leather jacket, and short crop top, showing off her navel.

"Out with friends," Arianna said.

"What friends?" I asked and stepped in front of her, pushing her gently back against the car.

"Friends, Kamden. I didn't know I needed to run them by you." Arianna blinked, planting her hands on her hips, causing her shirt to rise. I caressed her cheek, leaning in closer.

"Cancel and hang out with me."

"Nope."

"Why not?" I asked.

"That defeats the purpose of the bet. Unless you're forfeiting and going to give me a check for the charity," Arianna insisted.

"It's not a date, just two people hanging out."

She looked over at the house and back at me.

"I don't bite, well, unless we're in the bedroom."

"Funny."

"What do you have to lose? Hanging out with your girlfriends, listening to them complain about their boyfriends, or you can hang with me," I stated.

"That's not encouraging reason for me to go with you." Arianna pulled her keys out of her purse.

Chapter Ten

Arianna

"I'll drive your car and leave my bike here if you'd feel more comfortable."

He grabbed my keys out of my hands and opened the passenger door. I wanted to say something, but I liked this laidback side of him.

"This an official date?" I slid the seatbelt on, getting comfortable in my seat.

"Do you want it to be?"

I shrugged, not knowing if I wanted to go through with this or not. Kash was a cool guy, but it would be too much attention on me if we got into a relationship officially.

"Ari, try not to think too hard. Let's make a deal."

"We already have a deal with the race," I told him.

"Let's hang out and if you're having a terrible time, we can come back and not speak on it again and consider it an official bad date."

"What if we have fun?" I questioned.

"Then you owe me a date no matter who wins the race," he suggested.

"Mr. Coleman, you are really slick."

He chortled. "What can I say? I'm good at negotiating." Kamden started the car, turned on the signal, and pulled off into traffic. He turned the radio on to the local pop rock station and bobbed his head to Shania Twain.

"What?" he asked when he caught me staring at him.

"Where are we going?" I asked.

"Not too far from here, and you're dressed perfectly. So, don't stress about how you look," Kamden insisted. I looked at what I was wearing and back at him.

"I never do." I pulled the mirror down to check my makeup and saw him staring out of the corner of my eye.

"Stop staring," I said.

His eyes burned with lust. "You're beautiful."

"Thank you, and you're not too bad."

"Ohh, thanks. I guess," Kamden joked.

We stopped at the red light, and my phone rang, pulling us both from the shared stare. He answered the call without looking at the name.

"Hello."

"Baby, just listen," Freddie said, and Kash looked over at me. Before I could say anything back, Kash grabbed the phone out of my hand and hung it up. He placed it in his pocket and turned into Dave and Busters.

"Kash!" I screamed.

"We arrived."

"Can I have my phone back, please?" I asked and went to open the door, and he muttered under his breath for me to stop.

"When you're with me, I open all the doors, Arianna."

"Fine, but give me my phone back."

"When we're done, you can have it back," Kamden insisted.

I stepped out of the car and placed my hand in his as we walked inside to a small crowd of kids and parents. Kamden walked up to the hostess to get a table, and I followed beside him, taking a seat near the back corner of the restaurant.

"I didn't have you pegged as a Dave and Busters type for a date. I figured you would wine and dine me," I said, grabbing the menu.

"There's a lot you got wrong about me, Ari."

"Hi, I'm your server for the evening. My name is Tamela, can I get you something to drink first?"

"Can we get a bottle of Chardonnay and for appetizers, egg rolls, wings, and spinach dip? Then, I will order afterwards," Kamden said, taking charge of the night. I closed my menu and clasped my hands together, smiling at the waitress, not letting on that I was pissed.

"Great, I'll be back with your wine and appetizers," Tamela responded, leaving two straws on the table. Taking in the restaurant, I saw where a few kids played games with their parents, and other customers seemed to be on a date.

"Before you start, I apologize for ordering for you, but these are my favorites, and I wanted you to see me as Kamden and not Kash."

"What's the difference?" I asked.

He grabbed my palm, caressing it gently. Tamela came back with our drinks and appetizers.

"This is Kamden, the guy who hangs out at the Dave and Busters or with the boys at the house. When it's racing time, I turn into Kash."

"And hit up Vegas," I remarked, pushing a strand of hair behind my ear.

"Vegas or fly off to Dubai without telling anyone for a solo getaway."

I took an egg roll and dipped it in the sauce, biting down on the sweet flavors. I closed my eyes and moaned, ready to dive in fully. Tamela took out her notepad to take our dinner order.

"Can I get the ribs and fries please?" I asked, wiping my hands on the napkin.

"Sure, and you, sir?" Tamela asked.

"I'll have the same thing," Kamden answered, pouring the wine in my glass.

Honestly, I never claimed to be the type to let control go in a relationship and just allow a man to take care of everything when it came to plans, but Kamden was turning out to be funny, honest, and sexy. After eating our meal, we talked and eventually got up to go play some games. I won in basketball once and he won the race car game. Which he shoved in my face the entire night. Around midnight, we pulled back up to the house. When he got out of the car, I slid over to the driver's side and watched him start the bike.

"So, what did you think about tonight?" Kamden asked.

"I'll give you a B plus," I teased.

Kamden smirked, and I chuckled.

"I look forward to racing you, Ari." Kamden revved up the bike.

"Me too, Kamden. May the best driver win," I said, pulling off toward home.

Chapter Eleven

Arianna

Two *days later*

I enjoyed myself with Kamden, even though we never exchanged numbers. I wasn't too worried about not being able to get in touch with him. Today was the official day of me racing in the mainstream field. I was over the moon excited and couldn't wait to see my family's face when I crossed the line. I had my parents and friends cheering me on. Even my big-headed brother, Malik, finally came around to being okay with me racing. Cicely made a big breakfast, and Essence stayed over to make t-shirts with my number for the family to wear. My hair was pulled into a tight bun so the helmet would fit. I went over last-minute car checks with the pit crew to make sure everything was running fine. Now, I was grabbing a cup of water to calm my nerves when I felt a tap on my shoulder from behind me.

"Yes," I said, taking a sip of the water while wearing my suit.

"Stay away from Kash," a female demanded.

I glanced up at the ceiling, clenching my fists. I wasn't

stupid to think Kamden would be single and ready for a relationship. I myself wasn't completely into being in one but having one of his little sex buddies confront me pissed me off.

"Who are you?"

"Josie. I'm his girlfriend. I saw you two at dinner, plus in Vegas together."

"Are you stalking him?" I questioned.

She rolled her eyes and stepped in closer.

"We're together, and you need to stay away from him," Josie told me.

"When Kamden tells me that same thing, then I will."

"Josie," I heard Kamden call out.

"Kamden, baby. I was looking for you," she said sweetly, and I almost threw up in my mouth.

"Call me Kash. What are you doing here?" Kamden asked her.

"We were doing a special on today's race for the sports channel," Josie said.

"Then shouldn't you be with the other reporters?" Kamden retorted.

She was hurt by his comment and looked toward me. I shrugged, taking a sip of my water. Josie mumbled under her breath and stomped off.

"You all right?" Kamden asked.

I started to walk toward the garage to get ready before it started. Kamden grasped my elbow and pulled me into his chest.

"What, Kamden?" I put my palm on his chest, keeping distance. He took the cup of water out of my hand and took a sip. My mouth dropped open in shock.

"Josie is lying, whatever she says to you. I'm not her

boyfriend, husband, or plaything. It's been over for a while," Kamden said, passing me the cup.

"I didn't ask for an explanation."

"I know, but I want to make it clear. Good luck out there," Kamden stated, kissing me on the cheek.

"What just happened?" I muttered to myself.

Thirty minutes later, I was listening to the crowd cheer and clap for me. My family held a huge banner with my name and signs of good luck. I took slow breaths, just taking in the experience and this chance of becoming a full-time driver. I tightened my gloves and double checked my safety belt. I looked over at Kamden hitting the gas, revving up the crowd, and the flag flying back and forth.

"You got this, Ari," I said to myself.

The announcer came on and stated for everyone to leave the track, and the pit crew moved aside after doing one more check. I gave a thumb's up and listened to my team over the mic.

"Arianna, are you ready for this?" Jackson asked.

"I'm ready, Jackson. I promise I am," I replied.

"Make sure you leave them in the dust," Jackson told me, encouraging me with the family lingo.

Announcer: Five... Four... Three... Two... One... Go!

I sped off, keeping my grip tight on the wheel and feet on the gas, my pace steady and clear, not overthinking anything as a car came up to take the lead. I didn't panic and continued on, getting to the finish line coming in second place as the crowd cheered Kash on. I got out, took my helmet off, and waved to the crowd before thanking everyone on the team. A reporter called my name, and I walked over a little disappointed but ready to get back to driving.

"Arianna, how do you feel you did?" the reporter questioned.

I rubbed the sweat off my forehead with the back of my palm.

"I'm happy for my first time out on the track."

"You're busting barriers as an African-American woman in racing."

I nodded in agreement.

"I'm extremely excited and grateful for the opportunity and look forward to continuing on this journey."

"Does that include you and Kash Coleman officially being an item?" the reporter asked.

I laughed. "I don't talk about my private life."

"Well, thank you again, Arianna. We'd love to do a full interview with you at a later date?"

"Thank you, and I look forward to it," I said and walked off, meeting Cyrus and Reece near the pit crew.

"Ari! Oh my god, you were amazing," Reece said.

"Thank you. I appreciate the support, Reece."

"She's right, Ari. You did great out there for your first ride," Cyrus told me.

"Thanks, Cyrus," I said, and he winked.

"So, are you ready for our official date?" Kamden came up to us and wrapped his arm around my shoulder.

I removed his arm from my shoulder, not wanting any misconceptions with the reporters still around.

"Kamden, congrats, man," Cyrus said.

"What date?" Reece asked.

"A date she'll never forget."

"We can double it for a charity ride," I said.

"I don't mind a second bet, but you owe me this one," Kamden said.

"That's my cue to leave. Reece, are you coming tonight?" I asked.

"Yes, do you want me to pick you up?" Reece asked.

"I'll meet you there," I said and walked off toward my family.

"Honey, you did so good!" Mom said and hugged me tight.

"Thanks, Mommy. What do you think, Malik?"

He grinned and held his fist out for me to bump.

"You did good, Ari. I'm proud of you," Malik said.

"Thanks, Malik."

My dad kissed me on the forehead and gave me a hug.

"Mr. and Mrs. Pierce, nice to meet you." I stiffened at his voice while my parents looked at me and then him.

"Hello, Mr. Coleman," Mom said, smiling. *Is she flirting right now?* I thought to myself. Kamden extended his hand and lifted her palm up to place a kiss on it.

"Please, call me Kamden."

"Call me Chavonne, and this is my husband, Eddison," Mom said.

Jackson, Dad, and Eddison Jr. watched as Mom fell into a high school girl mode right before our eyes.

"Arianna, we're having a dinner to celebrate. You get to pick," Dad told me.

"Daddy, I appreciate the dinner, but I made plans with the girls to celebrate. Can I take a rain check?" I asked.

"Sure sweetie. Be safe and call me if you need anything," Dad replied.

I hugged everyone one more time before I headed back to change clothes and head home to get dressed for the club tonight. Maybe I'd even find a guy to take home and relieve some second-place sex.

* * *

The club was bumping. *Yonce* by Beyonce was playing, and Essence, Reece, and I were dancing in the middle of the floor. I felt good, the energy was fun and positive, no stress. My hair was down in curls, I was wearing gold shorts and a black crop top with gladiator heels. I was rocking large hoop earrings with full lips popping from the red lipstick.

"Go, Reece! Go, Reece!" I screamed. Reece was swaying her hips and bouncing her ass, showing off her curves.

"I'm glad Cyrus didn't come," I shouted over the music.

"Me too," Reece joked, and we slapped hands.

"Let's get a drink," Essence mentioned, fanning herself.

"Okay," I said, walking behind her, holding Reece's hand as we pushed through the crowd.

We walked up to the bar and ordered more shots and a bottle of champagne. Reece set up a VIP area for us, with a sign and balloons. The DJ even shouted me out when we got here earlier.

"On the count of three, we take the shots," I said.

"One, two, three!" Reece and I spoke.

My chest burned, and I felt even nicer from the shot. I asked the bartender for three bottles of water to go with the champagne.

"I'm ready to sit for a minute. I'm hot, and my curls are falling," I spoke up.

Essence nodded and led the way to our section. She started up the steps and paused, causing me to bump into her back.

"Essence, what's wrong?"

"Ummm, we're not alone," she said, and I looked around her at Kamden sitting in our section with Cyrus and some other guys.

A scowl crossed my face. I nudged her to get behind me, and I stomped toward him.

"Hey, there she is!" Kamden yelled, clapping his hands.

"This is my section that I paid for. Get out!" I snapped.

Chapter Twelve

Arianna

I tilted my head and tapped my foot, pissed as he sat there smiling at me like I was joking.

"Hey, baby," Reece said.

"Reece, it's girl's night. Leave Cyrus alone," I said.

She waved me off and sat on Cyrus's lap.

"What happened to girl code?" I questioned.

"I'm still your best friend, Ari. With the guys here, it means we save our money and spend theirs," Reece said.

"I like that logic," Essence said and came to sit between the two guys that I remembered were from Kamden's crew.

"Ari, you remember Tripp and Ralph," Kamden said.

"Hi," I said as I plopped down on the couch next to Kamden and opened the bottled water; my high was blown now that the men came to watch us.

Kamden leaned over and whispered in my ear.

"Stop pouting with your sexy ass," Kamden said as he kissed behind my ear.

I tried to keep my composure, but my upper lip lifted in a smile.

"Whatever."

"You can admit you're glad to see me. I won't hold it against you," Kamden stated.

"Arianna, I didn't get a chance to congratulate you earlier, but you looked good out there and right now," Ralph said, reaching out for a handshake. I looked at Kamden then Ralph and lifted my hand toward him, and he kissed the back of my palm.

"Thanks, Ralph."

"Yeah, thanks, Ralph," Kamden griped, and I slapped his shoulder for being rude.

Ralph smirked and walked back to his seat next to Essence. I noticed she was engrossed in conversation with Tripp.

"Let's get out of here," I whispered in Kamden's ear.

Kamden looked shocked, pointed at himself, and I giggled at his annoyance.

"I want you to take me home." I ran a hand up his thigh and squeezed.

"You sure that's what you want, Ari? If we do this, it doesn't—"

"Just sex. Nothing more," I finished his statement.

He lifted me up and put me over his shoulder when he jumped up, and I screeched in shock.

"Where are you two going?" Reece asked.

"To talk," I said, and Kamden slapped me on the ass, making me laugh. Kamden took me through the VIP exit in the back, gave his ticket to the valet, and finally placed me on my feet.

"You sure about this?" Kamden squeezed my ass, kissing the side of my neck.

"Yes."

"Here's your car, sir," the valet said as he passed him

his keys and attempted to open the door of the passenger side. Kamden motioned that he had the door and gave him a hundred-dollar tip. I sat and leaned over to open the driver's side door.

"Buckle up," Kamden said.

"Nice car."

"Thanks, baby," Kamden spoke once he got inside, then grasped my hand, putting it on his lap as he drove off.

We arrived at his condo forty minutes later. Before the door could even close, I was up against the wall with my legs around his waist as his hands roamed and groped my breasts. I arched my back in appreciation of his lips kissing up my chest after our shirts were scattered on the floor alongside my shoes.

"Kamden..." I moaned, pulling him closer into my chest.

"You always taste good, sexy," Kash replied.

"Fuck me now."

He trailed kisses up my throat, biting me lightly on my cheek.

"Just sex, right?" He questioned as he peered into my eyes. I didn't know what was happening between us or if I wanted something more. I could admit I wasn't ready to have another broken heart from a man.

"Only sex," I responded, and he nodded.

Kamden reached into his pants pocket for a condom, unzipped his pants, sheathed himself, and planted me on my feet to remove my shorts. I was glad I wore a thong and strapless bra for easy access without taking them off. Kamden kicked off his shoes. I grasped his face, forcing his tongue inside my mouth as he wrapped his arms around my waist and lifted me up against the wall, lining his dick with my entrance. He eased in just the tip, torturing me with pleasure. I scooted down a little to pull him in more, and he stopped moving.

"No turning back," Kamden commented.

"Okay," I whimpered in his arms.

"This is what you want... let me hear you, Arianna."

Kamden pushed in further and once again, I could feel him in my throat. He was so thick and long, I needed to catch my breath.

"Damn, you feel amazing, Ari," Kamden whispered.

"Don't stop... Ughh... Kash!"

His pumps were accurate and smooth as he took my left nipple in his mouth, going between sucking and licking.

"Yass!"

"Shit, let's take this to the bed," Kamden said as he walked off to the bedroom with his dick inside me. I heard him gasp as my sex clenched, paying him back for torturing me a few minutes ago.

"You're going to get it, baby," Kamden said and laid me down on the bed, pushing my legs toward the headboard.

"Hold them up and if you drop them, I'm going to eat your pussy until I have you walking funny at work," Kamden stated.

"That's not a bad thing," I responded, and he slapped me on the thigh gently, then rubbed the sting away with his lips.

"You'll see." Kamden slid back inside, circling his hips, stroking at an even pace.

"Ahhhh! Fuck!"

"I told you. Don't play with me, Ari... Mmmmm."

I noticed him watching me intently. His muscles retracted as his hurried strokes went slower and steadier.

A hot ache grew in my throat, and I couldn't tell if this was more than what we agreed upon. Crushing his lips to mine, I held my arms around his head and pulled him further into me as his body fell on top of me, and pleasure burned my thighs.

"Fuck! You're so good, Arianna."

"Mmmmm... Kamden." I sucked in a harsh breath, sliding a hand up his thigh and ass. He curled his fingers in my hair, then reached up and eased his hand around my neck, not too tight.

"You're... not... fucking anyone... else, right?" he demanded, and I shook my head in denial.

"Ohhh... Kamden!"

"Fuck, Ari, goddammit..." Kamden shouted.

He pulled out, stroking his dick, and I turned around, getting on my hands and knees. I craved the feel of his body enveloping me as he dove back deep inside.

"Ahhhhh... Yess... you feel so good." I gripped the sheets and pushed back into him.

Kamden kissed up my back, as I felt a surge of his strokes and lust crash into him, a battering ram to my gut.

"Come for me, Ari," Kamden said, and I nodded in answer.

The scent of our arousal kicked up my heartbeat another notch, and my orgasm washed over me in a skin-shifting, nerve-shattering dance.

"I'm coming!" I screamed and fell on the bed, and he pulled out and lay next to me, catching his breath. After a few minutes, he pulled me back into his arms and kissed my lips.

"I want to fuck you again, but I know you're sore," Kamden told me and gripped my sex.

"Ohhhh..." I stretched my legs to give him access.

"Let me run you a bath so you can relax first."

"I guess I'm not leaving anytime soon," I said as he got out of the bed and walked to his bathroom.

"Nope. No running out before morning either with a note," Kamden commented.

"I felt it was thoughtful," I said.

I heard the shower turn on and the door open, and he came over to lift me up in his arms bridal style and carried me to the bathroom. He gently placed me in the warm bubble bath, and I almost fell into a deep sleep from how wonderful it felt.

"I know you don't want your hair to get wet, so let me wrap it up in this towel for you," Kamden said, and I leaned forward. It was a sweet gesture, and I pondered if he did this for other women before.

"Are you getting inside?" I questioned.

"You want me to? I was trying to let you relax. I can't promise to have restraint in the tub."

"I'm okay with that." I grabbed the hand towel and squeezed the lavender body wash in the towel to wash my legs one by one. Kamden motioned for me to lean up, and he got behind me with my back to his chest.

Chapter Thirteen

Kamden

"What are you thinking about?" I asked.

"The race and tonight's events," she said, running the towel up my left, then right arm.

I grabbed the towel out of her hand and washed her back.

"You did amazing today. I wanted to kiss you right after the finish line but knew it would be a media circus."

"Your girlfriend would've been pissed," she said.

I dropped the towel and massaged her back.

"Josie's not my girlfriend. You know better than anyone that I don't do the girlfriend or relationship thing. I like being single. I'm still young, baby," I commented.

"Same," I heard her mumble slowly.

"Let's go to bed. I know you're still sore," I teased, watching her stand and grab the towel off the rack to dry off.

"The next race is for the charity event," Ari explained, walking in the bedroom, and I grabbed the body lotion off the counter and a towel. I followed behind her to the bedroom, squirting a small amount in my hand, and reached for her to prop her leg up on the chair in the corner.

"You ready for the race?" I questioned.

"Yeah, so get ready for round two." Ari watched me rub lotion on her arms.

"All right, racer, time for bed. It's past midnight, and I know you have work in the morning, and I have a hospital visit for charity tomorrow."

"What are you doing at the hospital?" she asked.

"I donated to the children's hospital for cancer research. They're doing the bow cutting for a new wing," I explained.

"Cocky, sexy, and funny with a heart for kids."

"Is that what you think of me?" I questioned her, opening the drawer and pulling a pair of boxers out.

She pulled the covers back and lay down, getting comfortable on the right side of the bed.

"You sleep nude?" I asked.

"Yep, is that a problem?"

"Nope, just be ready for me," I commented, as I stretched toward the nightstand, grabbed a box of condoms, and laid them on top, causing Arianna to chuckle at me.

"Good night, Kash," Arianna said.

I pulled her back to my chest, squeezing her thigh and kissing her cheek.

"Good night, racer."

* * *

A knock on the door let me know Cicely was here, and breakfast was ready. I ran a hand up Arianna's chest, grabbing her breast and turning her over, kissing her shoulder, cheek, and forehead. Her legs automatically opened for me.

"I haven't brushed my teeth yet," Arianna said, blocking her lips from me.

"I don't care," I replied, moving her hand and slowly kissing her lips. I groaned, feeling my dick get hard from the warmth of her sex.

"Mmmm... grab a condom, Kamden." Arianna rubbed my face, opening her lips further.

I pulled back and smiled, reached over to grab a condom out of the box, and pushed my boxers down. I lined up with her sex and pushed inside, feeling her walls choke my dick. I wiped the perspiration that trickled on my forehead and bent my knees, pulling her legs wider and grasping both sides of her waist.

"Have dinner with me tonight," I said, pumping at a steady pace.

Arianna arched on the bed.

"I... I... can't!" Arianna cried out.

"Tomorrow night," I whispered in her ear how her pussy felt so good. We went on for the next forty minutes until I filled the condom and passed out for another thirty minutes. Finally showered, we walked out of the bedroom redressed to eat breakfast. I held Arianna's hand, leading her to the kitchen when Arianna stopped in her tracks.

"Cicely," Arianna said.

"Arianna," Cicely said.

"What... What's going on? You know him?" Arianna questioned.

"She's my housekeeper, sometimes therapist, and second mom when I piss off my own mother," I told her, walking up to Cicely and kissing her cheek.

Cicely poked me in the shoulder, and I laughed.

"Wait, how long have you worked for him?" she questioned.

"Two to three months and yes, I knew you two were seeing each other. That's none of my business," Cicely said, putting two plates of bacon, pancakes, eggs, and an orange on the table.

"Is this going to be a problem?" I inquired with Arianna.

She looked at me and shook her head. "Why would it? We're not dating, right?" she retorted, taking the napkin and fork to cut into her pancakes.

"Right," I said and peered over at Cicely, who smiled at me.

Once we finished eating, Arianna left to go to work, and I left for the hospital and then to meet up with my mom.

* * *

"Mr. Coleman, thank you so much for coming today," Dr. Shelton said, shaking my hand. I was here with Sarai and Cyrus to dedicate the wing under my name and Cyrus Premier Enterprises. She was talking with the photographers and reporters, making sure they had the right angles and knew what questions to ask.

"Thank you for having me, Dr. Shelton. I know I speak on behalf of All Hands Homes and the partnership between Cyrus Premier Enterprises and my private donations we raised, helped to give the kids some hope," I told him.

"It really has. We won't keep you too long. Maybe sign a few autographs and photos," Dr. Shelton explained.

"No worries. Whatever you need, we'll be here," Cyrus said.

Dr. Shelton nodded and walked off with the nurses to prepare the kids for the surprise.

"You look like shit," Cyrus joked.

"Long night," I winked, flipping him off.

"If it was with who I think it was, make sure you don't fuck it up," Cyrus said.

"Nothing to fuck up. We're friends."

Cyrus didn't believe me and folded his arms over his chest.

"You don't even believe that. Hell, I said the same thing with Reece," Cyrus replied.

"Ha-ha, worry about your own situation. I'm good over here," I said, removing my shades and placing them in the sleeve of my leather jacket.

The doctor waved us over, and Sarai pointed for the photographers to start recording.

"Kids, we gathered you here to give you a nice surprise. We have some special guests that would like to meet you!" Dr. Shelton exclaimed.

"Yay... Yay!!" the kids cheered as we walked inside.

"How are you guys?" Cyrus asked.

"Good!" the kids screamed out, hugging their blankets and toys.

"I know you can do better than that. How are you doing?" I questioned.

"Good!! Good!" the ones that could, stood and clapped their hands.

"We came here because we wanted to give you guys a gift. Can we do that?" I asked.

"My friend, Kamden, has helped to provide the

hospital with resources to help you guys kick cancer's butt," Cyrus said.

"Also, I wanted to surprise you guys with a trip to the racing track when you feel better and the doctor says it's okay," I said. All the kids that could jumped up and ran toward us for a hug. The reporters rolled the cameras, and we took pictures and signed autographs.

Then we shook hands with some of the parents and did interviews with reporters.

"Thank you so much for spending your time with the kids. They love you guys," Dr. Shelton stated.

"Thank you for having us here. We love spending time with the kids," Cyrus said.

I waved goodbye and listened to Sarai tell me about my upcoming appearances.

"Your schedule is pretty clear, besides the charity event and race. You do a few club appearances and a photoshoot with the shoe sponsor," Sarai said.

"What day is the photoshoot?" I asked.

"They don't have an exact day. They'll work around your schedule," Sarai said.

"Let me look at my calendar and move some of the club appearances around. Maybe one or two a month," I responded, opening her driver's side door for her to get inside.

"Okay, just try to stay out of more fights with photographers," Sarai replied.

"I can't promise that. You know she set me up," I said.

"I could have told you that. Josie's always been sneaky." Sarai started the car and shut the door.

"Oops, I forgot Sarai is always right," I chortled.

"That's why you pay me the big bucks, Kash," Sarai said.

"Too much."

"Hey, don't say that aloud. Somebody might hear you." Sarai laughed.

She headed out of the guest parking and drove off back to the office. Cyrus came out of the hospital talking on his phone. He held his finger up for me to wait.

"Yeah, let me call you back," Cyrus said, ending his call.

"Was Sarai going back to her office?" Cyrus asked.

"Yep, and I need to get over to check on my mom and head to the gym to get a workout in before the next race," I said.

"Reece told me you were hanging at the house the other day. You good?" Cyrus asked.

"I'm good, don't worry. Your star driver isn't going back down the road of stolen cars anytime soon," I explained.

"Just checking in on you. The money and fame can go any day," Cyrus said.

"I got you, man," I said and drove to my mom's house.

I pulled up an hour later, and she was outside gardening in her yard. I parked in front of her driveway and removed my keys. I shut the door, walked up on her, and kissed her cheek.

"What's up, old lady?"

She scowled at me, and I cracked up at her facial expression.

"Sorry, beautiful."

"Grab a pair of gloves and help me plant these roses," she said.

"Where did you get roses from?" I questioned.

"A friend brought them over to me," she told me.

"What friend? Please, don't tell me you're dating?" I questioned.

"Maybe," she teased.

"Ughh... I'm going to be sick."

"Aren't you dating?" she questioned.

"Nope."

"Pass me the glass of lemonade, please," Mom said.

"Sure."

I passed it over to her before placing the gloves on.

"All right, where do I start?" I asked.

"Here, take the rose bed and plant them here."

"How was your day?" I asked.

"It was good. I went to the house and helped out Reece with the boys, ate lunch, and came home."

"Cool. I need to help Shane with his driving practice."

"How was the hospital?"

"Great. The kids loved the surprise and the photos," I said.

"That's good. Come inside and eat. I made some of your favorites," she told me.

"I'm still full from the big breakfast Cicely made."

I jumped up and helped her stand. She removed her gloves, and I left mine on the steps. She opened the door, and I walked in behind her.

"Go wash your hands, Kamden," Mom said.

"On it," I answered and headed to the bathroom.

As I opened the door, I felt my phone vibrate. I pulled it out of my back pocket and saw Josie texting me.

Josie: Can we meet up for dinner tonight?

Me: That's not a good idea.

Josie: Please, Kamden, just friends, like old times.

I sighed and thought it might not be so bad to have dinner with a friend since I didn't have any major plans.

Me: *All right, I'll pick you up.*

I turned my phone on silent to continue hanging out with my mom for the rest of the day until it was time for me to head to pick her up for dinner.

Chapter Fourteen

Arianna

Essence was driving the car, and I snapped my fingers to the beat of old school Janet Jackson's *Doesn't Really Matter* playing. We decided to go out to dinner and celebrate her promotion at work. After she got her master's degree, she applied to all the major companies in California for tech, and she was able to get a position as a lead tech designer for Temper, an app for parents with kids.

"This is my song," I said, swaying my hips in my seat.

"Get it, boo," Essence replied.

"You want to go to the club afterwards? I can see if Ree is free."

"I'm down."

"Okay, I'll text her when we get to the restaurant."

"Perfect, and we have arrived. Are you ready for the charity event?" Essence asked.

"Yep, I have a walk-through tomorrow with the designer," I said, getting out of the car where I stood waiting for Essence as she gave the keys to the valet. I decided to treat her to a fancy dinner at Giorgio's, a popular Italian restaurant. Frequented by celebrities, the only problem was that paparazzi hung around a lot. The maître d held the door open as we stepped in, giggling at her dancing in happiness about her new position.

"I'm really proud of you, Essence. You've wanted this for a long time," I said.

"Thanks, boo. You're doing amazing with coming in second place and then doing this huge event."

"Hello, welcome to Giorgio's. How many are in your party?"

"Two," I said.

"Great, follow me please," the hostess said. It was my first time inside Giorgio's. The vibe was little Italy with the atmosphere, and the colors were off white and cream, with vintage paintings and pictures on the walls.

"Oh," I said to myself about walking past the last person I expected to see.

"Here you go, ladies," the hostess said, placing our seat next to Josie and Kamden. I didn't know if I was on a hidden camera show or being punked. But I needed to keep my annoyance off my face. For someone to say they didn't have a girlfriend, and then attempt to ask me out to dinner, this was a new low I wouldn't even expect Freddie to do.

"Isn't this a small world?" Josie said.

"Uhm, can we move to another table?" I asked the hostess.

"Sure, of course," the hostess said.

Kamden jumped up to stop me.

"Ari, it's not what you think," he said.

"Essence, come on," I said, ignoring Kash.

"Kash, leave her alone. She's not worth it," Josie spat, and I turned around and pointed my finger in her face.

"Josie, if you want to keep your pretty little face, you'll keep my name out of your mouth."

"Are you threatening me?" Josie leaned back and folded her arms across her chest.

"You're not even worth it." I waved her off and tried to walk past, but Kash grabbed my hand.

"Kamden, let me go, please," I requested nicely.

"No, we need to talk," he responded.

"Nothing to talk about. Enjoy your date with your girlfriend, Kash," I replied.

"Fine, I will," he said and released my hand. I started to turn, when he suddenly bent down and picked me up over his shoulder. The timing was the worst because flashes went off from outside.

"Oh my god! Put me down, Kash," I said, slapping him on his back.

"It's Kamden. I told you that, Ari, plenty of times," he replied and pushed open the women's bathroom and walked in, not caring if anyone saw us.

"Are you crazy?!" I shouted when he put me down, and I poked him in his chest.

"You know the answer to that already, Ari," he said.

"Ughh! You get on my nerves," I said and stomped off toward the door. Kash blocked my way, and I planted my hands on my hips, waiting to see what excuse he came up with.

"Why are you so mad?" he questioned, and I couldn't answer that question. *Was I hurt because I was starting to feel something for him or was it because it was Josie? I thought to myself.*

"You're right, I'm not mad. Can I go now?" I asked.

"No," he said and grasped my face then covered my lips with his. I wanted to push him away, but at the same time, it felt so good to be in his arms. I grabbed his shirt and pulled him to me as we both claimed to be the dominant one with pent-up frustration.

I drank in the sweetness of his kiss.

"Mmmmm…" I moaned into his mouth as I went for his pants and unbuckled them.

"Wait, let me lock the door," Kash said and pulled away.

"Hurry," I said and watched him check under the stalls afterwards before he stood back in front of me, trailing kisses down my neck. I wore a low-cut, off-shoulder Versace dress. Not even taking the time to remove my panties, he ripped them off and tucked them in his pants pocket.

"I'm going to fuck that attitude out of you," Kash told me.

"I'd like to see you try," I sassed.

Kash lifted me on top of the bathroom counter and pushed my dress up, separated my thighs, and probed. With his other hand, he gripped the back of my hair, causing my head to tilt back.

"She's getting wetter for me, baby," Kamden said as he dipped a second finger inside, wetting it to spread the moistness around my clit.

"Kamden! Please, take me," I begged him, and now I couldn't wait any longer. I almost came apart when he pulled his fingers out and stuck them in my mouth and chased it with a kiss.

"We don't have much time, Ari. Keep quiet or I'll stop," Kamden told me before driving into my sex.

I shivered with pleasure as his eyes smoldered, and he

made the most animalistic sound I ever heard a human make.

At the sensuous touch of his fingers on my bare flesh, a low groan left my lips.

"Oh, God!"

He locked his mouth to mine and breathed life into me, I folded one leg around his waist, pushing him further into me. There was no more hiding from my feelings, and our fingers entwined in a tight grip.

"This convince you yet?" Kamden asked, as his palm drifted to my breast. He teased my nipples and sank deeper in me, forcing me to arch my back further against the mirror. I extended a hand behind me and met his strokes back-to-back.

"Yeah... Ahhh... Yes!"

I cried out as he slowly tongued my swollen nipple. He watched my pleasure as every nerve and cell strained toward him, and I melted into him. The heat around us intensified, and a knot of emotion burned in my center. A loud knock sounded at the door, but we never attempted to answer.

"Kamden... Ohhh."

"Give it to me."

"I'm coming," I said.

"Kash! What's going on in there?" Josie yelled.

"Nothing!" Kamden hissed, a tone that brokered no argument.

"Kash! Our meal is ready," Josie said.

"Fuck!" Kash yelled out, thrusting faster as I clawed at his back.

"Mmmmm... Okay... I believe." I chuckled as we gathered our breaths after a massive climax.

"You better, or we'll go another round," Kamden joked.

"We probably have a line outside waiting to get inside here," I replied.

Chapter Fifteen

Arianna

"I don't care what they want. Are we good?" Kamden asked as he kissed my lips, removed the condom, and tossed it away in the trash. He wetted some paper towels, cleaned his dick off, and got himself together. Then he wetted more towels and cleaned me off, helping me off the counter.

"Ignore Josie. She's not worth the headache," Kamden said.

"I hear you," I said, checking my makeup and hair.

He entwined our hands, headed toward the door, unlocked it, and we stood in front of Josie with a harsh glare across her face.

"You really stood out here listening to us?" I questioned.

"Kash, you need to make a decision right now. Either her or me," Josie demanded. Essence came over, and I felt even more embarrassed.

"Her," Kash said nonchalantly and walked off with me trailing behind, leaving her mouth gaped wide.

"Kamden! Wait. She has a boyfriend. I bet she didn't tell you," Josie insisted.

The flashes went off again as we approached our table, and I just wanted to go home, shower, and change. I was no longer in the mood to eat and celebrate with Josie following us around.

"For your information, Josie, Freddie is not in my life. Even if he was, that's none of your business or Kamden's for that matter," I spat as I grabbed my purse and dropped Kamden's hand to walk out before I further embarrassed myself over a lover's quarrel when he wasn't even my man.

"Arianna, don't walk away from me," Kamden told me as he wrapped his arm around my waist and pulled me into his chest.

"Where are you going?" Kamden whispered in my ear.

"Home."

"I'm going with you."

"Fine, then hurry up with your little friend. If you're not out in two minutes, I will leave without you," I spat.

"And I'll find you. Stop with the attitude," he stated, kissing behind my ear.

He released me and smacked me on the ass. I rolled my eyes and left behind Essence laughing at me as I rubbed the sting out of my ass.

"That wasn't funny," I said, blocking the flashes of the cameras.

"Over here, Arianna! Over here!" A member of the paparazzi requested.

"How was dinner with your boyfriend, Arianna?" a second reporter in flip flops and a cell phone probed.

"Dinner with friends, that's all," I replied, waiting for the car. I focused on Essence as they surrounded me.

"Come on, Arianna, tell us the truth," the first paparazzi wearing an FMZ shirt and wide-lens camera taunted.

"Here's your car, ma'am," the valet stated to Essence. I ran to the passenger side of the car, jumping inside, lowering the seat back to hide.

"Take me home, please," I said.

"What about your man? He just walked out looking around for you," she questioned and honked her horn.

"Essence!"

Kamden tapped the window for me to roll it down.

"I'll follow behind you, Essence," Kamden said.

"I can just text you her address," Essence said.

I jerked back in shock.

"Uhm, what makes you think I want my address given out?" I questioned.

"You should remind me next time before I hear you moaning because of him," Essence remarked, taking the car out of park and heading toward my house. I peered through the side mirror and noticed Kamden driving in his car behind us.

* * *

Essence parked in my driveway, leaving the car running.

"Are you coming inside?" I asked, unbuckling my seatbelt, and opened the door.

"Nope, I'm heading to find a man to slide on top of."

"How am I not surprised?" I said.

"Says the girl who smells like sex. That bathroom soap didn't work, boo." Essence smirked.

I just shook my head, closed the door, and turned to find Kamden waiting on my doorstep. Trudging toward my house, I pulled my keys out and stayed silent. Hearing Lucky barking, I stepped inside and bent down to pick him up.

"You missed me, baby?" I asked, rubbing his stomach.

Kamden closed and locked my door, while I walked toward my bedroom to shower and change.

"You can stay out here; I'm going to shower."

"Ari, don't start. I was just inside you. That's childish to ignore shit," Kamden said.

"I'm not ignoring you. We'll talk as soon as I get out."

"All right." Kamden sat on the couch, and I planted Lucky down on the floor, and he ran to Kamden, snuggling against his leg.

"Traitor," I mumbled under my breath.

"Don't be mad because he likes me better," Kamden chuckled.

I swayed to the bedroom, opening the door. I removed my dress and dropped it in the closet with the other dry-cleaning clothes I needed to take care of tomorrow. I walked to the dresser drawer and picked out tights, a big t-shirt, and underwear. Opening the bathroom door, I placed my clothes on top of the toilet, turning to pull the shower door open. Once the water heated up, I stepped inside and decided to wash my hair at the same time. I grabbed the towel and oatmeal soap to wash my body when I felt a breeze from the door opening, and Kamden stepped inside, naked.

"Let me wash your hair, baby, since I fucked it up," Kamden chortled.

"Since I fucked it up," I muttered, repeating his words, and he laughed even harder.

"I love your hair," Kamden said.

"Thank you," I responded.

He squeezed the conditioner in his hand, rubbed it together, and scrubbed his hands through my hair, making me feel cared for—a foreign feeling outside of what I got from my family.

"Josie won't bother you anymore, I promise."

"You sure promise a lot of stuff."

"What she said about your ex, is it true?" Kamden questioned.

"No, he's tried to get back with me, but I told him I've moved on," I answered as I turned the water off then adjusted around to face him.

Kamden grasped me around my waist while I leaned into him, running a finger across his bottom lip. He opened his mouth and took my finger inside, biting it gently. Wanting to show him that he wasn't the only one who could cause a craving when he was away, I slid down slowly and lifted his dick as it twitched at my touch. Kamden let out a low groan as I took his erection in my mouth all the way to the back of my throat. He shattered into millions of pieces as a flick of my thumb slid across the tip of his thick erection when I pulled back. I licked him from the mushroom head down to the base of his pubic hair.

"God, Ari! You're fucking beautiful, baby," Kamden grunted out.

"Mmmmm..." I moaned.

While I sucked him, I pushed a finger in my wetness at hearing the way he was crumbling under my hold.

"All right, that's enough," Kamden demanded, tapping me on the shoulder.

I grinned, continuing my torture by twirling my tongue around his head, and finally popping him out of my mouth. Stroking him faster, letting a little saliva fall onto his erection, I watched his eyes darken as lust fell over him as he turned bright red.

"Fuck this," Kamden snapped and picked me up. I cackled at him as we stepped out of the shower slowly so as not to fall. He picked up the two towels off my rack and walked back to my bedroom. He placed the towels down and dropped me on my feet.

"Get on your knees," Kamden demanded.

"I haven't finished, Kash," I taunted as I crawled up on the bed.

"I don't care. You're not doing that with anybody else, I swear to God."

"What are you asking me, Kamden?" I questioned, watching him spread my legs with his and line his dick with my entrance.

I closed my eyes, feeling him move slowly back and forth.

"I want you to be mine, Ari," Kamden insisted.

"Are you asking or telling?" I asked, catching his rhythm.

"Whatever gets you to say yes." Kamden slid out and bent down to eat my pussy as I came.

"Yes! Oh God. Kamden, I'm yours," I screamed from another orgasm. I fell on top of the sheets and turned over, watching as he laid next to me and wrapped his arm around my waist.

"Go to sleep," Kamden said.

"We still need to talk," I said.

"Tomorrow. You wore me out, girl," Kamden joked.

I chuckled and tried to shove him away. We both burst into laughter and kissed on the lips as I pulled the throw blanket at the edge of my bed over us before falling into a deep sleep.

* * *

The next morning, I woke up in an empty bed and looked around to notice Lucky sitting on the edge near his doggy bed. I sat up against the headboard and wondered where Kamden went without letting me know. I stood, walked to the living room naked, and found my purse to check for messages.

Kamden: *Hey beautiful, I didn't want to wake you. I had to get to a meeting with Cyrus.*

Kamden: *Don't pout.*

Kamden: *I still can taste you on my lips.*

Kamden: *For real, stop pouting. You left me a note the first time.*

I giggled at his last text and sent one back.

Me: *You're not that funny. I'm working today at Pierce and doing a walk-through of the venue.*

Kamden: *Sounds good. Let me know your plans for lunch.*

Me: *I can't promise, but hopefully, I'll be at the track for practice.*

The three bubbles went in and out, signaling that he was thinking of what to say next.

Kamden: *All good, talk soon, sexy.*

I put my phone on charge and went back to the bedroom as Dreamy followed behind me to the bathroom so I could shower and get dressed. Cicely set out the food so she must have done it before I came home last night; everything was neat and tidy. Forty minutes later, I came out of the bedroom dressed in a sleek, light-blue pants suit and black heels with a white button-up shirt. I decided to keep my hair down and flat with minimal makeup besides mascara, lip gloss, and moisturizer.

Chapter Sixteen

Arianna

I parked in my normal employee space, turned the car off, and jumped out with a cup of tea from my favorite coffee and tea shop with a cinnamon raisin bagel in my hand. I walked through security, scanning my badge, and smiled at Glenda, the receptionist. She'd been with the company since Jackson started a few years ago. Falling in line with the other two women, we entered the elevator, and I asked for floor fourteen. The doors closed, and I took a sip, taking a look at my watch as the door made it to my stop. I headed to my office to gather the final details to present to Jackson. Reece was meeting me at the venue to do a walk-through and report back to Teddy.

"Morning, Arianna," Tisha said.

"Morning, Tisha. How are you?" I asked.

"Good. I saw the race. Sorry I missed it."

"No worries. Are you coming to the charity ride?" I asked.

"With bells on," Tisha replied.

"Awesome! Can you meet me in my office so we can run through my schedule?"

"Yep, let me grab my notepad," Tisha answered.

I opened the door of my office, gasping in surprise. The entire room was filled with flowers. I was completely thrown off. Tisha came up behind me and stood in shock.

"Wow," Tisha said.

"You didn't know about this?"

"No. Who do you think set this up?" Tisha asked, walking toward the red roses sitting on the glass table.

"I can guess one name," I mumbled to myself.

"You think it was Kash?" she asked.

"Is it that obvious?"

"Pretty much every day, I get an alert about a sighting of you two." Tisha bent down to smell the flowers. I groaned already, feeling sick to my stomach that people would hound me like they did the other night at the restaurant.

"You shouldn't listen to gossip, Tisha," I cautioned.

"Normally, I don't, but I'm a huge fan of Kash's." She sat in the chair in front of my desk, and I pushed the glass vase of roses to the corner of the desk. I dropped my briefcase to the floor and made sure not to drop my tea and bagel. Landing in my chair, I sighed, feeling exhausted from the night before and wondering how long it'd take to clean out all the flowers.

"Can you call the shelter on Third Avenue to see if they'd like flowers?"

"You're not keeping them?" Tisha questioned.

"You can take some if you want. I'll take the vase home later today. Everything else can be donated."

"He likes you," Tisha stated.

"I like him too even though we started under unusual circumstances," I replied.

"Well, I see more than like, but we can save that for another day," Tisha joked.

"Funny, but we have a full plate of details to go through. Let me log into my computer."

Typing in my password, I found the file for the charity drive with Pierce and Cyrus Premier Enterprises as co-sponsors.

"So, we have how many invites sent out?" I asked.

"My list has four hundred. This doesn't include fan tickets," Tisha said.

"Do you think we should cut down the personal invites?"

"I think the more the better. Most likely, people won't show up, and maybe put RSVP as another check off," Tisha explained.

I pulled the file folder with all the details out of my briefcase.

"Okay, let's do that, and you'll have to manage things with Reece while I'm driving. Afterwards, I'll go change and meet you at the venue for the after party."

"Food is ordered, and we'll have chicken, fish, and steak as the main dishes people can pick."

"Probably should keep it at two items. Too many choices will drive the chef crazy."

A knock on my open door caused me to smile, and I invited him in.

"Hey, sweetie," Dad said.

"Hi, Daddy. When did you get here?" I stood, walking around my desk to hug and kiss him on the cheek.

"An hour ago. I was on a conference call. What's going on here?" Dad pointed around at the flowers.

"Would you believe me if I said I like flowers?" I chuckled.

"Looks like someone is trying to replace me." Dad pouted, and I smiled, standing on tippy toes to kiss his cheek again when he bent down. Both my brothers got their height from him.

"Never that," I replied.

"What are your plans for lunch today?" Dad questioned.

"I have a meeting at the venue for the charity race."

"I was going to treat you to lunch like old times. We didn't have our monthly date," Dad told me as he wrapped his arm around my shoulders.

"Sorry about that. I got slammed with work."

"And some boy named Kamden. But that's okay. Let him know to come by the house for dinner so we can officially meet," Dad said.

"Isn't that old school, Pops? You never did that with Eddison's wife or all of Malik's women."

"Eddison's wife did have dinner with us, but you were too young to remember. Malik is a lost cause in the love department," Dad joked.

"You're a mess, Pops. I'll take a rain check on lunch and call you tomorrow to set up a date for us."

"Sounds good and don't forget I want to dine with that boy, Kamden," he told me.

"Yes, sir."

Dad winked, waved at Tisha, and walked out of my office. I walked back to my chair and continued going down the list of things that needed to be double checked for the event.

"Is the DJ hired?" I asked.

"Yep, and he's fine with mixing old school with newer

age music. I know some of the kids from the house will show up," Tisha said.

"Yeah, I want to make sure it's not too crazy, but they won't be there long," I replied.

I added in more notes, and we checked off the upcoming calendar of events.

"Okay, do you need me for anything else? I can get started on calling the shelter," Tisha stated.

"No, that's all. If anyone calls for me, take a message," I said.

"Sure," Tisha responded and left my office.

Putting away closed files from past events, I added in more details of the color scheme for the cake decorator and then decided to call Kamden. I took my phone out of my purse and speak of the devil, he was FaceTiming me.

"You left without saying goodbye?" I questioned as I rubbed my hair down into a ponytail.

"You left a note. This ain't *Sex and the City*, baby," Kamden joked.

I cackled at his response, joking about the breakup post-it note that Carrie got from Big.

"Whatever."

"What are you doing?" Kash asked.

"Working at the office on some last-minute details for the charity race."

"What time are you leaving today?"

"Uhm, probably about one. I need to check the venue out with Reece and then go shopping," I said.

"I'll meet you at the mall. Which one?" Kash asked.

"Aren't you too famous to hit up the mall like us little people?"

"I'll wear shades and a hat," Kamden told me.

"Okay."

"We can do lunch afterwards," Kamden said.

"Oh, that reminds me. My dad wants you to come over for dinner. No pressure," I said.

"I can do that, and you can come to dinner with my mom," Kamden answered.

"You don't think it's too early to meet the parents?"

"We both know how short life is for us in this sport. Stop trying to put barriers up, Ari."

I milked him, and he caught me and blew a kiss through the phone. I laughed, and we continued talking for the next five minutes until Ralph called for him in the background.

"I'll talk to you later; I need to see what he wants," Kamden told me.

"Okay. Bye."

We hung up at the same time, and I relaxed in my seat, staring up at the painting on the wall of a young woman looking out into the ocean. It was called a *Searcher*, and I think I'd been searching all my life for something or someone that could match me in every way. But Kamden was a little different and spontaneous in a way that I didn't need to worry about him expressing his feelings. His actions showed. Freddie needed me to lead him into his passions, never really showed me love unless it was to complain about something my family did. If you couldn't stay up and fight for me with my family, then you couldn't fight for me in the world. I continued working on my next proposal to present to Jackson before it was time for me to leave and head out for the day. Closing out of my computer and grabbing my purse, I walked out of my office and told Tisha I was leaving for the day.

* * *

I waved at the coordinator as I parked and stepped out of my car. She recommended the Sofitel Hotel for the dinner afterwards, and I agreed if the space was able to hold the amount of people we were expecting and red carpet.

"Hi, Reece, Arianna," Delores said, extending her hand.

"Hi, Delores. Thanks for squeezing this meeting in. I know you're busy. I won't keep you long."

"Hey, D," Reece spoke.

"You're good. This is party number ten we've done together. You get the VIP treatment," Delores stated.

"Thanks, girl."

The doorman held the door wide for us to go through, and I pulled my shades off to look around at the space.

"This would be the entrance after everyone walks in from the red carpet. They come here for check-in and interviews," Delores stated.

The layout was gray and white with specks of black and gold. The lobby held a registration station and sitting area with artwork and standing sculptures.

"You said they would give us the pool area, right?" Reece asked.

"Yep. If guests want to head to the pool area for a nightcap, we'll have parts of it blocked over the pool for people to dance on top of the pool if they wish."

"Nice. How many guests for dinner?" I questioned, talking behind her to the meeting manager of the hotel.

"Hi, Arianna. Nice seeing you again, Reece," Julia, the manager, said, and Reece waved hello.

"Hi, Julia. I was wondering if you'll be able to hold up to a thousand people."

"We have two rooms we can combine plus the lobby,"

Julia told me. I nodded in answer as she opened the party room.

"Okay, this looks good. I'd like to have the decorations match the team colors. Maybe the waiting staff could have ties that match each team," Reece advised Delores and Julia.

"Great idea," Delores said, taking notes.

"I can't stay long. I have lunch plans, but I trust you, Delores, and I'll see you at the event."

"Perfect! If I have any questions, I'll let you know, but Tisha and Reece have been great with keeping things on track," Delores remarked.

I placed my shades back on, shook Julia's hand, and hugged Delores before walking out with Reece to head for lunch.

Chapter Seventeen

Arianna

His stare was bold, and he assessed me, frankly. I blushed, kissing him on the cheek as Reece walked into Macy's; we trailed behind. Kamden wore shades and a baseball cap to cover up his identity. Reece picked up a dress to model for me, and I shook my head, releasing my hold on Kamden's waist.

"What about this red dress?" I asked.

"Cyrus will go ballistic," Kamden said, shaking his head no.

"Why? It's cute," I replied.

"Ari, that dress is too short, baby," Kamden said.

"Men have no sense of fashion," I told him.

"I agree with you," Reece said, looking through the rack of designer evening gowns.

"I'm wearing black, and I think Essence is going in blue," I said.

"Okay. Let me try this gold dress on and maybe a few of these red dresses. Cyrus will have to survive," Reece teased. I chuckled and watched her walk off toward the dressing room. Kamden checked out the suits, and I walked up behind him.

"I want you to be my date for the charity dinner," Kamden said.

"You know the paparazzi will be there plus reporters."

"I know, and I'm ready for the media circus. Wonder what name they'll give us," Kamden joked.

"Kari!" I blurted out, and we laughed together when I heard a throat clear. I turned and saw the same three women from the beauty shop.

"Can I help you?" I questioned.

"Kamden, I missed seeing you at the club," the Brittney girl said, ignoring me.

"I'm not sure why you're looking for me," Kamden told her.

"We had a date, remember? Candy was there when you asked me out," Brittney stated, trying to make me jealous.

"I'm here with my girlfriend. I don't know you or remember asking you out," Kamden announced.

"That's a lie!" Brittney shouted as she stomped her feet.

"Uhm, excuse me, do we have a problem over here?" the store employee asked.

"We're trying to shop, but they're interrupting us," I hissed.

"Bitch, I'll do more than interrupt you," Brittney spat, stepping in my face.

"You really don't want to do this," I said.

"Kamden, you're acting funny now, but a few weeks ago, we slept together, and you promised to call me again," Brittney stated.

Kamden, looking pissed, clenched his fists.

"Let's just go," I said.

Reece walked out right on time because when I turned, I felt a hand grip the back of my head, and I screamed in pain.

"What the hell!" Kamden shouted. I punched Brittney in the gut with my elbow, and she released my hair. I tried to punch her in the face, but Kamden picked me up around the waist, and I kicked and screamed to be put down.

"What just happened?" Reece asked.

"His little girlfriend tried to fight me," I shouted.

"I don't even know her, Ari," Kamden pleaded.

"Put me down!" I screamed as the girls walked out behind us, trying to egg me into a fight.

"Ari, let it go. They're not worth it," Reece said.

"Can you put me down, please?" I asked Kamden.

"Better that you run now! I hate to see you on a gossip blog going to jail," the Candy girl shouted.

I tried to break out of his hold and run toward them, but Kamden held me tight around my waist. They laughed, and I noticed the third girl recording us. I wanted to flip her off, but it would only cause more unwanted attention.

"I need to get out of here," I said.

"We can go back to my place," Kamden told me.

"No," I said, removing his arm from around me.

"You don't believe her, do you?"

"Reece, let's go," I told her. We headed out of the Beverly Center Mall when a slew of paparazzi snapped our photos. I bet all of them were working together. Hiding my face, I went toward his car since I parked at his condo. Getting inside after he opened the door, Reece slid in the backseat, and Kamden drove through the crowd of fans and paparazzi that noticed him.

"I'll get Sarai to handle it," Kamden told us.

"Yeah, another scandal for her to clean up for you," I sassed, crossing my legs and sitting closer to the door, avoiding his stare. If I did a Google search, I would probably find a lot of shit Sarai had to get cleaned up. Kamden turned on Melrose and drove home as his phone rang back to back.

We pulled up to his place twenty minutes later, and I hopped out, heading to my car. Kamden snatched the keys out of my hands before I got inside and held them over my head.

"Reece, take her car, and she'll call you later," Kamden said.

"Really, Kamden, you're so childish," I said as he bent down to kiss me on the lips.

"That won't help you. I'm still pissed about your little girlfriends."

"Don't blame me because they lied to get a reaction out of you," Kamden said.

"Are you good, boo?" Reece asked.

I flipped him off and hugged Reece. "I'm good. We'll talk once I'm home," I said.

"Okay, call me later," Reece said as she picked up the keys from Kamden and got inside to drive off.

"Hungry?" Kamden questioned as we walked into his condo building.

"Is this funny to you?" I asked.

"Ari, we can't control those types of women. You know that better than anyone."

"At least acknowledge that your past or probably

present isn't helping right now," I said watching him hit the elevator for his penthouse.

"Are you forgetting how we met?" Kamden reminded me.

"I remember, and I left you a note, not looking for anything long term. Do not flatter yourself."

"Sweetheart, calm down. You're getting worked up for no reason. Fuck those girls," Kamden said.

The doors of the elevator closed, and he pushed me up against the corner, kissing me on the lips, taking my breath away.

"Mmmmm..." I moaned as I wrapped my arms around his shoulders.

"Fuck, you taste so good. They don't compare," Kamden said.

"Glad you know that. So, don't fuck this up," I said, pointing between us right as the doors opened.

"I gotcha, racer," he said, calling me by the nickname he gave me.

He opened the door for me to walk in, and I kicked off my shoes and jacket and walked to the kitchen to grab a bottle of water. I heard someone talking, and Cicely came from the back, talking on the phone.

"He just arrived. I'll let him know," Cicely said.

"Who was that?" Kamden questioned, watching Cicely put the house phone on the charger.

"Sarai was checking to see if you guys made it home safe," Cicely informed him.

"I'll call her back later," Kamden said.

"What happened?" she asked.

"Some of his girlfriends tried to fight me, and photographers just happened to be there," I said as I rolled my eyes. Cicely walked over and lifted my chin to check for bruises.

"You all right?" Cicely asked.

"Yep."

"I'm heading to take a shower," Kamden stated.

"Are you hungry?" Cicely asked us.

"We're heading to dinner at her parents' place."

"We are?" I asked, shocked at his statement.

"Yeah, I'm tired of you doubting us, or do you want to meet my mom for dinner?"

"Maybe better to head to your mom's place. If it's all over the news about the fight, I'd rather not deal with answering questions."

"You'll love his mom," Cicely commented.

"I can hear my brothers screaming about me fighting over some man," I fussed, sitting on the island chair as Cicely cleaned up.

"Eddison probably wouldn't fuss as much as Malik," Cicely said as she pulled the dishes out of the sink and dried them off.

"Malik needs to stop playing all these women and settle down." I took a sip of water.

"Just like Kamden, right?" Cicely inquired.

"Yes, old wise one," I joked, and Cicely narrowed her eyes at me.

"Wise and still sexy at my age," Cicely remarked and stuck her tongue out at me.

"Cicely, the last thing I want to hear is you talking about being sexy." I pretended to gag.

"Girl, ask your momma if I can still pull a man. Even though I don't want them."

Fifteen minutes later, Kamden walked into the living room wearing fresh clothes.

"Cicely, why are you talking to her about dating? The only man who should be on her mind is me," Kamden said, kissing the side of my forehead. I rolled my eyes and noticed Cicely smirking at me.

"I'm glad you two found each other," Cicely said.

Kamden reached over and entwined our palms.

"Ready to head out?" Kamden questioned.

I nodded in answer, waving bye to Cicely. Kamden told me he was close with his mom, and I hoped she accepted me. If she didn't, I wondered if Kamden would continue seeing me. Kamden held the door open for me as we exited his condo and walked to his car.

"What's going on in your head?" Kamden asked.

"Nothing."

He swung me around and pushed me up against his car, pressing his body against mine.

"What's your favorite color?" Kamden asked.

"What?"

"What's your favorite color?" he questioned again.

"Baby blue."

"What pisses you off? Makes you happy, turns you on?" Kamden asked.

"Where is this coming from?" I questioned, folding my arms.

"You have insecurities, Ari. I can see it in your eyes. I know you portray this strong woman who takes no shit. But you're afraid of not being loved," Kamden said.

I chuckled and looked away at his comment. He thought he was fixing something broken in me.

"I don't need fixing, Kamden. I'm not some scared, insecure person."

"You sure about that?" he asked.

"Yes."

"So, why are you letting that chick get into your head?" he replied.

"I'm—" I started to say and stopped, avoiding his eyes. Was I insecure about being with him? Was this what Freddie felt like when we were dating?

"I get it, Kamden. Maybe I went a little overboard, but I have a feeling they'll keep trying to do something to break this up. Whatever this is," I told him, standing on tippy toes to kiss his lips.

"Josie and any other girl can say what they want. I know who I want to sleep with at night and wake up next to in the morning," Kamden said, stepping back to open the door.

"Who would that be?"

"A spoiled woman named Arianna Pierce," Kamden joked.

We both laughed at his comment as I slid inside the car, and we drove off toward his mom's house.

"Black," Kamden spoke, startling me from my thoughts.

"Black what?" I replied.

"Black is my favorite color. I was raised by a single mother. In and out of trouble with the law when I was younger, and some say even to this day," Kamden talked as he drove.

"I was pretty much a book smart and street-smart type of kid. I was spoiled, but I worked my butt off with good grades and have been working since I was sixteen," I explained.

"I've never had a girlfriend, until now. So, it's expected that I'll make mistakes," Kamden said.

I jerked back at his comment.

"Expected?" I questioned, pushing my ear closer to hear his response.

"Baby, I'm saying I won't cheat on you. Sometimes, it's more than a sexual connection. Emotional distance because of work," Kamden informed me and leaned back in his seat.

"I hear you."

He peered over at me and smiled before turning onto the 101 Freeway into traffic to take the long drive to his mother's place. An hour later, he pulled in front of her place and shut the car off.

"Anything I should know about, so I'm not caught off guard?" I asked.

"Just be you. I promise it's not all bad," he joked.

"Well, I can't say the same for my family," I responded, watching him get out of the car and walk around to my side and open the door.

I lifted my head to meet his gaze, and he smiled back at me.

Chapter Eighteen

Kamden

I pushed my hair behind my ear, stretching my arm around her shoulder as we stepped up on the porch of my mom's house. The door opened, and my mom smiled wide when she noticed Arianna.

"Kamden, who do we have here?" she asked.

"Ma, this is Arianna Pierce, my girlfriend," I replied, and Ari looked up at me in shock.

"Girlfriend. Well, you come inside. I didn't expect another person for dinner, but I can throw another steak on the grill." She stepped aside to allow us inside, and I closed the door behind us.

"Arianna, nice to meet you! My son has never brought a woman to meet me," Mom said.

I groaned at her statement and rubbed a hand up Arianna's back. I motioned for her to take a seat on the couch. I moved toward my mother and kissed her cheek as she headed to the kitchen.

"So, Arianna, what do you do?" Mom called out.

"I work in event planning, and I recently started driving," Ari said.

"Really, you are?" Mom asked.

Ari nodded in answer.

"Your parents aren't scared?" Mom questioned.

"My family knew I'd always wanted to be a race car driver when I was younger, and my cousin owns Pierce Motors, so it's kind of in my blood," Ari answered.

"That's right. You came in second place at the race a few weeks back," Mom stated.

"She lost a bet that if I won, she had to go on a date with me, and if she won, she could name any price for me to donate to the charity," I informed my mom.

"Are you driving in the charity race?" Mom asked, coming into the living room with two glasses of wine.

I took it out of her hands and passed to Arianna.

"Thank you," Arianna stated. "I am. I'm also planning the dinner. Are you coming?" Ari asked.

"I normally stay home and watch the race; it's too much for me to watch in person. For this one, I'm coming," Mom said.

"You'll get to meet my parents," Ari said.

"That's perfect. So, tell me, what do you see in my son?" Mom joked.

"He's not that bad," Ari replied, rubbing my thigh.

"See, I'm not that bad."

"Well, I'm happy for you two. Arianna, anytime you want to come over without him, you're more than welcome," Mom told her.

"Thank you, Ms. Coleman," Aria stated.

"You're welcome. Let's eat," Mom told us. Ari and I stood and left for the dining room. I held the chair out for Mom, then Ari.

"This looks good, Ms. Coleman," Ari informed my mom.

"Thank you. Do you cook, Arianna?" Mom questioned.

"I do, not every day, but with Cicely, she keeps my fridge full," Arianna said, picking up her napkin.

"Oh, that's right. Cicely is your housekeeper and Kamden's," Mom announced.

"Yes, it was a surprise to find out," Arianna stated.

"Don't worry, she doesn't tell all your secrets," Mom joked.

Arianna glared at me, and I shrugged, not looking to get involved in gossip.

"I'm joking, Arianna. She hasn't told me anything about you besides you're a wonderful woman, and your family is close and well known in the community," Mom replied.

Arianna let a weight off her shoulder and relaxed while she continued listening to my mom talk about me growing up and even brought out the baby pictures during dessert. We left around nine that night, and I drove back to her house for the night.

* * *

"Mmm... fuck!" I hissed then squeezed my eyes tight as I felt a warm mouth on my dick. I licked my lips and popped my eyes open as Arianna pulled my dick out of her mouth and palmed it with her tiny hands.

"Come here," I demanded.

"I wanted to surprise you before I left for work," Arianna said.

"I want to fuck you so bad, Ari," I groaned, trying to control myself. I buried my face in her neck, squeezing her thigh. She captured my lips, grinding on top of my dick.

"I need to get dressed for work. Kam... oooh!" Arianna moaned when I eased her down on my girth.

"We won't be long," I whispered, then lifted her gown over her head, tossing it to the floor.

"Ahhh... damn." Arianna bit her bottom lip as she squatted down with her legs wide open, bouncing up and down.

"Yeah. Keep going," I grunted as I raised my hands to grope her breasts.

"Tell me this is real, Kamden. I need to hear you say it," Arianna asked aloud.

"I can show you better than tell you," I stated and switched positions with her and placed her up further in the middle of the bed with her legs pushed toward the headboard. I lined back up with her sex and felt my dick pulse the moment I tapped the head against her pussy lips. I lowered myself, kissing on her neck as I pushed inside her walls. We both gasped in response. *I am falling in love with her,* I thought to myself.

"Oh God!" Arianna mumbled.

My heart skipped a beat when I looked over at her beautiful face. She reached around and grabbed my ass, pushing me in further.

"I want to fuck you every day. Every night, I want to make love to you and be with you forever, Arianna Pierce," I announced as I stared into her eyes. I saw a pool of tears fall down her cheek. I kissed each tear.

"I want you too," Ari answered.

"You're so wet, baby." I met her gaze.

I bent down and bit her nipple. She sucked in a breath as my tongue flicked across each nipple. I thrust as echoes of our moans settled in the room. I didn't hear her dogs barking so she must have put them in another room before waking me up.

"Yessss! Fuck me, please," Ari screamed as she dug her nails in my back.

I could tell her orgasm was coming at full speed, and I gripped her waist with both hands. I'd apologize later if I left her sore.

"Oh shit! Arianna, come for me, baby," I growled.

A few minutes later, she screamed, shaking in my arms as I continued stroking her through the orgasm. I was out of breath but slowly pumped in and out, feeling my release leave my body. I was exhausted and ready to go back to sleep. I rolled over, trying to catch my breath.

"Damn," I muttered.

"Damn," Arianna said, and we both chuckled.

I reached down and palmed her stomach and rubbed up and down.

"We didn't use protection, Kamden," Arianna mentioned.

"I know, but I always get tested. I can show you on my phone," I stated.

"I have my papers in my nightstand. I'm clean," Ari answered.

"I trust you," I said, kissing her chin. "We both need to get dressed," I commented.

"Ughh, I know. I have a few calls, and then I was planning to visit my mom," Ari said, getting out of bed and walking to her bathroom. I stood naked and stretched, checking my phone to see a message from Cyrus asking that I get a practice in today before the event.

Cyrus: *You have the track if you need to practice.*

Me: *Cool, I'll be over soon!*

Cyrus: *Gotcha.*

I heard the shower running, and I put my phone back down and turned the TV on right as network news *Daily Morning Show* posted a scrolling screen of us at the mall yesterday. I turned up the volume a little to hear.

"We have superstar racer Kash Coleman trying to break up a fight," Linda Aliza stated.

"Can you believe it, Linda? This time, he's breaking up a fight and not in one," Paul Landstone replied.

"Fuck," I mumbled.

"We see two women, one is speculated to be Arianna Pierce, the daughter of Eddison and Chavonne Pierce and cousin to the owner of Pierce Motors, a billion-dollar franchise," Linda mentioned.

"According to his publicist, it was a misunderstanding by a fan," Paul said.

"Doesn't look like a fan interaction to me. How many times have we seen him with different women every other day?" Linda implied, chuckling. I squeezed the remote when I heard Arianna call out for me to join her.

"We hope he's trying to get his life on track. He just won the race a few days ago, and a bigger one is coming up. We'll continue to watch to see how this story ends," Paul said.

I turned the TV off and walked into the bathroom, shaking my head. The shower door was open, so I stepped inside and walked up behind Arianna, kissing the back of her neck.

"I'm sore, Kamden. Move, you're not slick. You can wait for round two tonight," Arianna whined.

I laughed at her response and lifted my hands in surrender.

"I promise, baby. I just wanted a hug," I answered, holding my hands out wide.

"Hmmmm... I see that little smirk on your face," Arianna said as she grabbed the towel to wash my chest. I kissed her forehead and cheek as we washed each other up. An hour later, I was leaving her place with the same clothes I came in last night. I ran to my house to get changed and finally made it to the track to get some time in for practice. I parked my car, heading inside, and noticed Tripp standing off to the side of the garage.

"What are you doing?" I asked. He motioned for me to be quiet, and I leaned further over his shoulder and saw what he was watching. Josie and Ralph were arguing back and forth.

"What's up with that?" I whispered.

"I don't know. I just got here a few minutes before you and heard loud arguing," Tripp said.

"She's his problem now," I said.

"Good, but I have a bad feeling about them after he got in her face more, and then she set up that paparazzi photo here," Tripp said before he turned to head back inside.

"Don't stress yourself out. How's everything looking for practice?" I asked.

"Good. I haven't seen any issues since the last ride."

"Cool. I'm doing a few laps today."

"What's up with Arianna's friend?" Tripp asked.

"Who?"

"Essence," Tripp said and smiled.

"Honestly, I have no clue. Every time I see her, she's by herself."

"Tell Arianna to put in a good word for me," Tripp said.

"I'm not getting involved with that, man. They call me a playboy and cocky. Your ass is the biggest hoe around the track," I joked, and Tripp flipped me off.

"So, you're a reformed hoe now?" Tripp questioned.

"Something like that." I took my jacket off and placed it on top of the work bench.

"What, are you and Arianna in a relationship?"

"I made it official earlier today," I said.

"Wow! Kamden Kash Coleman off the market."

"Please keep it to yourself. I saw it on the news this morning about the fight the other day. I didn't tell Arianna," I said.

"You should; you don't want her out here blindsided," Tripp replied.

"I know, but the way she looked so content in my arms, I didn't want to change her mood. I'm meeting her parents for dinner," I replied.

"Really? Meeting the family time."

"We had dinner with my mom, so it's only right she introduces me to her family," I responded.

"It's ready to go," Tripp said.

"Cool. Have you seen Cyrus today?" I asked.

"He was up in his office doing an interview," Tripp said.

"I'll talk to him later."

The car was rolled out to the track, ready to go, when Josie noticed me and started to walk over. I held my hand up to stop her from dampening my mood.

"Save it, Josie. I'm working, and you know when I'm in the mood to drive," I said.

"Kamden, it's not what you think. Ralph was just doing an interview with me," Josie lied, and I let her continue talking behind my back.

"I don't care," I said nonchalantly.

"You used to care!" Josie shouted, shoving me in the arm.

"Exactly, used to. I don't anymore and have fun with my leftovers, Ralph!" I shouted as he glared at me.

Josie huffed and walked off. I ignored his stare, not wanting to get into a fist fight before the big drive came up. I'd hate to put him on his ass. We used to be close but ever since Josie sank her nails into him, things had changed between us.

"You good?" Tripp yelled, and I nodded, pushing on the gas, signaling I was ready to go. I took a few laps around the track, pulled over, and turned the ignition off. Leaving the car, I took my helmet off and passed it to Tripp.

"How's she running?" he questioned.

"She's ready," I stated and smiled, bumping fists with him.

Chapter Nineteen

Arianna

Dinner at my parents' was tonight, and I was nervous. It was a day before the big charity race, and my nerves were all over the place. Kamden told me about the *Daily Morning Show* talking about the fight I was in, and my lawyer got a phone call from a woman talking about suing me. I scoffed at the audacity to try to get money out of me when she was the one who started the fight.

My niece and nephew ran around the room yelling and screaming. Reece and Cyrus came over to help smooth any tension in the room if things got out of hand. Both of my brothers came, and Malik brought some new girl I hadn't met. I doubted he was serious since the second she opened her mouth, it was all about our family and how we lived and being celebrities which we didn't claim to be. Jackson had bodyguards if he was taking the family on a trip, because he was well-known out of the country. The door rang, and I jumped up and ran to the door, pushing my nephew behind me. I let out a deep breath and opened the door to Kamden holding a bouquet of flowers. I smiled, moved to the side to let him in, and reached over for a kiss.

"You made it on time."

"I told you I would," Kamden said.

"Who are you?" my nephew asked as he pointed at Kamden with his thumb in his mouth.

"Major, this is my friend, Kamden." I bent down until I was eye level with my nephew.

Kamden did the same and stuck his hand out toward Major.

"Hi, Major. I'm Kamden."

Major grinned with a wide smile and shook Kamden's hand. We stood, and I took the flowers out of his hand.

"Kamden, you didn't run?" Reece joked.

"Reece, stop scaring the boy," Mom said.

"That's okay, Mrs. Pierce. I don't scare easily," Kamden stated and winked at me. I blushed, covering my face with my hands. He reached over and pulled me into his chest.

"How are you, Kamden?" Mom asked.

"I'm good. Ready for the big race," Kamden replied. His eyes lifted when my father walked into the living room from the back. Cicely even came over to help my mom set up dinner for tonight.

"Mr. Pierce," Kamden said, extending his hand for a shake. I watched my father look at his hand, glance over at me, then back to Kamden.

"Kamden, nice to see you again," Dad said as he returned the shake.

I let a long-held breath go and relaxed.

"Are you ready for dinner?" I asked.

"Starving, sweetheart," Kamden said.

"Who is this, sis?" Eddison Jr. asked, sounding just like his son.

"This is my boyfriend, Kamden," I said.

"Ohhh, you were serious," Eddison Jr. joked, and I punched him in the arm.

Kamden looked at me, perplexed.

"Ignore him." I grabbed Kamden's hand, and we went to eat dinner as a family.

"Don't eat the mashed potatoes," Cyrus whispered low to Kamden.

"Why?" Kamden asked.

"Essence wanted to join, and she made the mashed potatoes. Let's just say they're not fully where they need to be," I stated. Cyrus and Reece burst out in laughter when we walked out to the backyard to Essence and Cicely setting the table.

"Hey, Kamden," Essence called out.

"Nice seeing you, Essence."

"You, too. Try not to get my girl in another fight please, especially when I'm not there," Essence told him, and I waved her off, putting those events behind me.

"All right, that's enough. We're having a family dinner," Mom said.

"Kamden sits here, and Cyrus is next to Reece," I said.

"Oh my god! You're Kash Coleman," Malik's friend screamed out, jumping up and down before she rushed toward him.

"I am, and you are?" Kamden asked.

"Penny. Can I have a picture?" Penny asked.

"Sure," Kamden said.

"No!" Malik and I screamed at the same time.

"No pictures tonight, Penny. Sorry, you have to find someone else to harass," I blurted out.

"Excuse me?" Penny retorted.

"Girl, sit," Reece chastised.

Essence and I laughed at Reece.

"Malik, are you going to let them talk to me like that?" Penny questioned.

"Yeah, Reece's like a little sister to me. You act like you've never seen a celebrity before," Malik told her.

"Fine." Penny pouted and sat.

"EJ, where's your wife?" I asked.

"She had an event to cater. I said I'd take the kids with me," he said.

"So, Kamden, what are your intentions with my daughter?" Dad asked.

"Hopefully, to continue dating and see where it takes off. I like to live in the moment and not rush anything," Kamden said, reaching over and rubbing the top of my palm.

"My daughter doesn't play second fiddle to any man. So, make sure you keep your past in the past and the women under control."

"Daddy," I muttered.

"This one right here is mine. My baby girl, and when she is disrespected or hurt, you'll have to deal with me. Don't worry about her brothers. It's something I should ask about," Dad informed him, his face stern.

"Eddison!" Mom shouted.

"Ma, you know Pops is right. Ever since she met him, Arianna's been in a non-stop drama," Malik stated.

"That's not true, Malik," I said.

"Arianna, it's fine. I'm overprotective of my mom, so I get what they're saying," Kamden said.

"So, we're clear," Dad said.

"Arianna means more to me than my own life. Yes, we met in Vegas, but neither of us were looking for anything serious. Over time, things changed," Kamden commented.

"Kamden makes me happy, and I've explained to Kamden how I feel about his past lifestyle," I confessed.

"Just remember you're dealing with more than just Kamden. The industry to social media already dragged you through the mud for fighting over a man," Malik spat.

"Malik, you're just like him if you ask me," Reece mentioned, taking a sip of her iced tea.

"I can speak for Kamden and say he's come a long way, Mr. Pierce, and is just like me. You gave me a chance when you met me and opened your home," Cyrus told my dad.

"If Cyrus vouches for you, then I guess you're good. Just remember what I said," Dad told Kamden.

"Always," Kamden replied.

"Arianna, pass the mashed potatoes," Essence said. Everyone at the table froze at her statement.

"Huh." I played like I didn't hear her.

"Pass the mashed potatoes around so everybody can try them," Essence said.

"Uhm, I'm good, sis," Eddison Jr. stated.

"Me too," Cyrus spoke up.

"Make that three," Reece said, gulping down her iced tea.

"Madison, do you want some mashed potatoes?" Essence asked my four-year-old niece.

"No," Madison replied.

"Why not?" Essence probed.

"Gross. Don't make me eat it, daddy." Maddison teared up, and the entire table burst into laughter.

"Little girl, there's nothing wrong with my food. Auntie Chavonne, you want some?" Essence questioned.

"Sweetie, I love you so I will keep it real with you. Your potatoes look like soup and taste like raw eggs," Mom explained, and I groaned as Essence's face dropped in shock. Malik and Eddison Jr. slapped hands in laughter.

"Stop laughing, Malik," I said to take up for Essence.

"Arianna, you didn't put any on your plate?" Essence questioned.

"Remember, I started a new diet—no carbs," I said.

"Cicely, it's not that bad, is it?" Essence inquired.

"Baby, I must agree with Chavonne. You can't cook for shit," Cicely answered, passing the salad around. They cooked a big barbeque feast of ribs, burgers, hot dogs, spaghetti, lemon cake, baked beans, and green beans.

"Kam—" Essence started to ask, and Kamden held his palm up, stopping her.

"Essence, I'd prefer to stay on your good side," Kamden said.

Essence jumped up, grabbed her mashed potatoes, and stomped off toward the house.

"See what y'all did? Now I have to hear this for the rest of the week," I spat.

"At least you don't have to eat it," Reece joked.

"Reece!" I cackled at her joke.

Fifteen minutes later, Essence came back and sat.

"Sorry, friend," I said, getting up and walking over to whisper in her ear.

"You're good." Essence sighed.

"You must have tasted it," I commented, and she nodded her head.

I shook my head at her and sat back down to eat and talk with my family about the race.

Three hours later, I was in bed, riding Kamden backwards as his hands spread my ass cheeks, watching me take all of his thick length.

"Keep going!" Kamden yelled.

"Thank you..." I moaned out.

"Shit, Ari!" I bounced harder, grabbing Kamden's ankles and bouncing faster.

"I appreciate you, Kash."

"Fuck! I'm coming, baby," Kamden grunted and before I jumped up, I felt him release inside me. I fell back on the bed and felt myself drift off to sleep.

* * *

Charity Race

Finally, it was time for me to solidify my name in the racing world. The crowd chanted and roared as the drivers lined up. I looked over at Kamden, and he smirked back at me. Reminding me of where those lips were a few hours earlier. We'd had a rocky ride since we met, and now this was the moment we'd both waited for. I glanced at the patch with my last name sewn across. My entire family was in the stands watching me. Even my niece, nephew, and sister-in-law who rarely had time to get out because of her business as a chef were in attendance. I waved as my family held signs with my name and number across them. A few feet below, I noticed Josie sitting in the stands. I found that strange; usually she'd be out doing interviews. Sarai asked if I wanted to do some interviews for magazines, and I said I would even if I didn't win. I was still flying high from the dinner at my parents' house.

Nothing would derail my dreams. The announcer called for silence.

"Ladies and gentlemen, please stand for the national anthem," the announcer said.

Everyone stood with their hands across their hearts as a local twelve-year-old sang. We all clapped for support. I double checked my helmet and gloves before jumping inside the car while the pit crew stood off to the side. Essence stood with Tripp, and I found that odd since she hadn't talked about knowing him outside of briefly meeting him at the club. I pumped the gas as the adrenaline pulsed through my blood. I closed and opened my eyes, breathing slowly, and looked to the right of me and saw Ralph smiling at me. I shivered at the fakeness and made a reminder to tell Kamden after the race to have a talk with his friend. Taking off, I listened and talked with my team through the headset and focused on nothing else but the finish line. I kept a steady pace, not overpowering like the last race. I watched as one car passed me, and I bit my bottom lip. As the curve came up, I pumped the gas full force and kept both hands on the steering wheel taking a lap around. I was still in the top three cars and almost running out of time. Tasting the finish line as we came up on the last lap, I released a long-held breath and pushed myself even further and passed the other two drivers and finished first.

"Oh my god! I won!" I screamed while the team congratulated me through the headset. When I tried to slow down, the brakes didn't work.

"Ugh... guys, something's wrong," I said.

"Arianna, listen to me and breathe," I heard Cyrus through the mic.

"Cyrus, something's wrong," I reiterated, trying not to panic.

I continued to try to push the brake pedal, nothing happened.

"Ari! What's going on?" Kamden asked.

"Kamden, the brakes won't work!" I cried out.

Suddenly, the car started smoking and caught fire.

"What the fuck!" I heard Kamden shout.

"Get her out of there!" Cyrus yelled.

BOOM!

The car rattled and exploded as more smoke came through. I felt myself slip away then everything went black.

Chapter Twenty

Arianna

Three days later

I felt a heaviness weighing me down, as loud voices went back and forth. I groaned trying to lift my hand, but my eyes were too heavy. I felt my name being called, and I mumbled slowly for some water. My throat was raspy and dry.

"She's awake!" I heard someone shout.

"Get the nurses!" I knew that was Dad's voice.

"We're here, Ari. We've been here." That was Reece.

I wanted to open my eyes, but I drifted off again into a deep sleep.

A few hours later, I finally opened my eyes fully and looked up to see Reece and Essence sleeping on the couch together. I tried to pull myself up an inch or two and saw Kamden sitting in the chair next to my hospital bed. I picked up the nurse's button and a few seconds later, a nurse and a doctor came inside and turned the lights on.

"Glad to see you awake, Arianna. I'm Doctor Erwin." His voice caused Kamden, Reece, and Essence to wake up.

"Where are my parents?" I questioned.

"They went to get food in the cafeteria," Essence said. Right as she said that the door opened with my parents and brothers walking behind them.

"My baby," Mom yelled, running toward me as the doctor continued to check my vitals while Dad stood at the foot of the bed, rubbing my feet. I looked around the room, nervous about what was happening.

"How do you feel?" the doctor asked.

"Sore all over," I said, sighing.

"That's expected. You had a pretty bad crash."

"What—"

The door flew open with Freddie busting inside with balloons and a teddy bear. Kamden jumped up and charged at him.

"What the fuck are you doing here?" Kamden asked.

"Man, get off me," Freddie said.

"Kamden, let him go," Mom muttered.

"You might as well leave. Her real man is here," Freddie spat.

"Arianna, you need to tell me something?" Kamden asked.

"Both of you need to leave," Malik yelled.

"She hasn't talked to you since I've been with her, so I suggest you leave, bro."

Freddie chuckled at Kamden's statement.

"And if I don't?" Freddie questioned.

"Then we can take this outside," Kamden told him.

"Kamden, please stop," I spoke hoarsely, feeling myself getting dizzy.

"All right, you both need to leave. You're making her blood pressure go up," the doctor stated as he rechecked my pulse and heart.

"Get off me, man!" Freddie shouted then pushed Kamden until he let go. Kamden pushed him back and swung at him. Malik jumped in the middle of the scuffle, and my dad and older brother tried to pull them apart.

"That's enough!" Mom screamed, clapping her hands.

"Kamden!" I screamed, and he pushed my brother back.

"Motherfucker, you lost your mind!" Malik shouted, punching Kamden in the face.

"Oh my god!" I cried.

Dad was able to put Freddie out of my room as Kamden and my brother went blow for blow. The nurse called for security and broke everyone up.

"I want everyone out of her room now," the doctor demanded.

"I'm not leaving," Mom advised him, her hands on her hips.

I nodded at the doctor to allow her to stay while the rest of my family was asked to go to the waiting room.

"What about the baby?" Kamden loudly questioned.

Shocked by this question, Kamden and I were going to be parents. *Do I want a child right now?* I thought to myself. We had not used a condom in a while, even though we had a slip up that one time at my place.

"What are you talking about?" I asked.

"We can talk about it later, Arianna. You've had too much stress," Mom said.

"No, tell me what's going on."

"You've been unconscious for the past few days. You came in with a broken hip bone, cuts, bruises, and a head injury. We ran tests, and you're three weeks pregnant," the doctor commented. I looked over at Reece and Essence for confirmation, and they both nodded.

"Ari," Kamden called my name.

"Tell her, Kamden. She needs to know the rest of the story," my brother said.

"What else?" I questioned, staring into his eyes. I laid back on the bed, rubbing my temple.

"The car crash wasn't an accident. It was intentional," Malik informed me, glaring at Kamden.

"Wait." I held my hand up.

"Malik, you could have waited to tell her when she was out of the hospital," Essence insisted.

Kamden grasped my hand, and I snatched it away.

"What are you talking about?" I gritted through my teeth.

Kamden sighed and ran a hand down his face.

"Ralph was arrested for tampering with your car. Josie came to me afterwards and told me. They're still investigating but brought him in for questioning," Kamden explained.

"Let me guess, she happened to confess this detail out of the kindness of her heart," I quipped.

"Baby. I failed you once, but I promise. Moving forward, your safety is my priority," Kamden told me.

"That's not happening," Malik demanded.

"You have no say in our relationship," Kamden said.

"I have to agree with my son this time, Kamden. The people you surround yourself with obviously have some-thing against my daughter," Mom said.

"Mrs. Coleman, I promise she's in good hands," Kamden said.

"Kash, can you leave please?" I said.

"Kamden," he stated.

"What?"

"Don't push me away by calling me Kash. You know me better than anyone," Kamden stated.

"I need space please," I answered.

"It's getting late, and she needs rest," the doctor said.

Kamden peered into my eyes, looking for any trace of my love. After the news of Ralph setting me up to get killed, I couldn't trust him.

"Okay, I'll leave for now. But we will talk soon," Kamden said and leaned down to kiss me on the lips. I turned my head, and his lips landed on my cheek. Kamden looked brokenhearted, and I wanted to apologize, but my emotions were all over the place.

"Arianna, we'll be back tomorrow," Essence and Reece said, walking out behind Kamden.

It left me with the doctor and my family.

"Did the crash affect my baby?" I asked.

"No, the baby is strong. You're both lucky," he replied.

"Thanks, Doc," I said.

"I'll let you get some rest, and we'll talk more tomorrow."

The doctor shook hands with Mom and Dad, then headed out with the nurse behind him.

"You're staying with us when you get out, baby," Mom told me.

"I don't want to put you both out," I said.

"You're our child. Never say anything like that again," Dad told me.

"So, I'm going to be an uncle?" Eddison Jr. asked.

"I don't know," I muttered.

"What do you mean?" Mom questioned.

"Nothing, Ma."

"Arianna, listen to me. What happened is not your fault or Kamden's." She held her hand up to stop me from interrupting her.

"The person to blame is the one who messed with your car. Am I disappointed in Kamden? Yes, but at the end of the day, the person who did this is in jail," Mom told me.

"Ma, you're too forgiving. Kash played with that girl's heart, and she manipulated that dude to kill Ari," Malik remarked.

"Malik, shut up. Arianna is grown and if she wants to date him, it is her business," Mom replied.

"Even if she becomes a single mom?" Malik insisted.

Mom shrugged her shoulders. "Arianna will never be alone."

"Daddy, what do you think?" I asked.

"Baby girl, I think you need to give it some time. I am not saying he's a problem, but you're always caught in some mess with him," Dad told me. I agreed with a nod and slid down lower in bed with the thin blanket around me.

"Can you turn the light off on your way out?" I asked, ready for bed.

"We'll be back in the morning," Dad and my brothers said as Mom got comfortable on the couch, and we both dozed off for the night.

Chapter Twenty-One

Arianna

Four days later, I was discharged and back home with my parents. Cicely was helping out, and she decided to sleep in the guest room to be close. She also brought my dogs with her. I was lying in bed watching TV with Lucky and Dreamy beside me. I changed the channel from another *Real Housewives* reality show to a repeat video of the car crash on the *Daily Morning Show* with my name scrawled across. I turned the volume up.

"This is the actual video police are using to investigate the car wreck that race car driver Arianna Pierce, was involved in at the charity drive," Linda said.

"Looks like it was a combination of things happening, Linda, and she's lucky to be alive," Paul replied.

"I agree, Paul. Our sources say she was unconscious for a few days before waking up and going home today. Her publicist informed us that she thanked everyone for their well wishes." Linda then read off a statement that Jackson had prepared through Sarai.

"The police have a person in custody, and what's shocking is it's a fellow driver, Ralph Cox," Paul stated.

"Some even say it's a lover's quarrel, and that she was dating both Ralph and Kamden," Linda lied.

I groaned, shaking my head at the way the media manipulated stories of people in the public eye. The camera cut to a video of the police taking Ralph into custody with a huge crowd of photographers surrounding him, trying to get a statement. I turned the volume down when I heard a knock at the door, and Cicely stepped inside with a tray of food.

"I thought you might be hungry," Cicely said, putting the tray down across the bed.

"Actually, I'm not," I said, not having an appetite since everything went down.

"Well, you need to eat for the baby, Arianna," Cicely fussed.

Agreeing, I picked up the fork and pushed the scrambled eggs around on the plate. She knew my favorite meal was breakfast anytime of the day. Right now, it was going on one in the afternoon.

"What are you watching?" Cicely asked.

"The news," I replied.

"Why do you torture yourself with that crap?"

Cicely walked around my room, picking up the clothes thrown around since getting discharged. It was still decorated like a sixteen-year-old's room with posters and my favorite color, baby blue. Last time I was here, I slept over after hanging out later after dinner and not feeling up to driving home. Now I might be here for the next few weeks until I was completely healed. Jackson for sure wasn't letting me back on the racetrack, and Cyrus put me on leave of absence. Thank God Reece was able to get the charity event refunded and everything canceled, although people still donated knowing everything that happened to me.

"I was scrolling through and saw my name pop up."

"It won't do anything but keep you and the baby stressed, Ari," Cicely fussed.

I picked up the glass of water and sipped.

"Have we seen him?" I questioned.

"No," Cicely said.

"He's not home?"

"Don't get mad. But he hasn't been home since you kicked him out of the hospital."

"Typical," I spat.

"He's just as hurt as you, Arianna."

"I doubt it."

"You think he wanted this to happen? He feels guilty, and to find out you're pregnant made it even worse," Cicely explained.

"Do you think I'm wrong?" I questioned.

"I can't tell you how to feel," Cicely answered.

"What would you do?" I asked, watching her put my clothes in the bathroom hamper.

"I would take my space and clear my head. At the same time, I wouldn't let misdirected hurt and pain dictate who I choose to love," Cicely said.

"Thank you, Cicely."

"For what?"

"For being a friend," I said.

"You're welcome, baby. Now eat so my little munchkin can grow big and healthy," Cicely teased, rubbing me on the shoulder.

She walked out of the room, and I continued scrolling from channel to channel and eating when my phone vibrated. I picked it up off the nightstand and saw a group text message from Essence and Reece.

Essence: *How are you?*

Me: *Hey, y'all. I'm fine.*

Reece: *Are you sure?*

Me: *Yes, I promise.*

Essence: *Do you need anything?*

Me: *Lol! New parents.*

Reece: *They put you on a punishment with no visitors.*

Me: *Seriously?*

Essence: *We tried stopping by yesterday.*

Me: *What did they say?*

Reece: *You needed rest.*

Essence: *I even tried to bribe them with food.*

I burst into laughter and typed back.

Me: *What did you make?*

Reece: *Please don't get her started.*

Essence: *Reece, you said it was good!!*

Reece: *I lied to spare your feelings.*

Me: *What was it?*

Essence: *Spaghetti and meatballs.*

Reece: *The meatballs were still frozen.*

Essence: *They were Italian style.*

Me: *What's Italian style, Essence?*

Reece: *Please, explain that.*

Essence: *It's a new thing on TikTok.*

Me: *You made a meal from a TikTok video?*

Essence: *All right, when you say it like that, it doesn't sound right.*

Reece: *That was the edible part.*

Me: *OMG, are you okay, Reece?*

Reece: *Barely, and the boys said Essence isn't welcome at the house.*

Essence: *Shane smiled when he tasted it.*

Me: *He probably wanted to spare your feelings, boo.*

Essence: *Whatever.*

Reece: *Lol! We still love you.*

Essence: *Anyway, when can we see you?*

Me: *I'm here if you want to come pick me up.*

Reece: *Shower, and we'll be over soon.*

Me: *Sounds good.*

I clicked out of the messages when I received a notification. I clicked on the tag and saw Kamden in Vegas with some friends in a club, drinking. Shaking my head, I tapped into my contacts and blocked his number. I got out of bed and went to my closet to grab some clothes to dress in for the day. Grabbing a jogging suit and sneakers, I walked to my shower and placed the items on top of my counter. He was out living his life like nothing had happened, so I'd do the same thing. I knew I couldn't trust him with my heart, then he had the balls to fight Freddie in my hospital room like his ass was so squeaky clean. I turned the water on and checked the temperature before jumping inside with my shower cap on to keep my hair from getting wet. I scrubbed my body twice over, seeing the bruises slowly clearing up with some scars that might take longer. The doctors said they could do plastic surgery, but I didn't know if I wanted to go that route just yet. I heard a knock on my bathroom door and called out.

"Yeah!"

"Arianna, Reece and Essence are downstairs," Mom said.

"Okay, tell them I'll be down soon."

"Don't overdo it, Arianna. You're still recovering," Mom told me.

"I'll be careful."

"Okay." I heard her say.

Twenty minutes later, I strolled out of my bedroom wearing shades, a hat, and a purse. I was still sore, so walking from point A to B took me a little longer.

"You look like shit," Essence blurted out.

"Thanks, Essence," I responded as I rolled my eyes.

"You're welcome," Essence remarked.

"Where are you going, ladies?" Mom asked.

"The park; the boys want to play basketball, so I thought I'd see if Ari and Essence wanted to tag along," Reece told her.

"That could be good, getting fresh air," Mom replied.

I hugged Mom and squatted down, putting Lucky and Dreamy on their leashes to bring them with me. Essence grabbed Dreamy, and we headed outside to Reece's car.

"Will we all fit?" I asked.

"Yeah, Jackson has the boys already at the park," Reece said, getting in the driver's seat.

"Where's Cyrus?" I questioned.

"Vegas," Reece stated.

"That's just perfect," I said.

Reece sighed and put her seatbelt on.

"I know it's not ideal, Ari, but I'd prefer Kamden didn't do anything stupid. So, Cyrus decided to go with him," Reece confessed.

"How long have they been out there?" I questioned as she drove off, then stopping at the stop sign.

"Right after you kicked him out of the hospital room," Reece said.

"They keep replaying the crash repeatedly. I can't escape," I confessed.

Reece pulled into the park a few minutes later and turned the car off.

"I think you both need some time apart," Reece said.

We stepped out of the car and walked over to the boy's playing basketball. Jackson was sitting on the bench, talking on the phone. Reece waved at him as we walked over and hugged him.

"Hold on one second," Jackson told the person on the other end.

"Hi, Jackson," I said.

"How are you, Arianna? I heard what happened. The boys wanted to make you a cake when they found out you were in the hospital," Jackson stated.

"That's sweet, but I'm fine."

"Good. I'll let you ladies have some privacy," Jackson said and continued with his phone call as he headed to the boys on the court.

"So, what's your plan?" Essence asked.

Sitting next to Essence, I let Dreamy and Lucky off their leashes, and they ran around the boys.

"About what?"

"The baby," Essence replied.

"At first, I was surprised, still am honestly. But this baby is a blessing."

"So, I'll be Auntie Essence, throw a huge party, and cook," Essence said.

"Slow your roll, Essence. I'm only a few weeks along. No reason to try to poison me with your food."

"I plan on getting Ivy to help me if you must know," Essence snapped and waved us off. Reece and I laughed at her pouting with her lip poked out and arms crossed.

"I'm glad you're keeping the baby, Ari. Kamden was worried. It's the main reason he took off to Vegas, to drink his problems away," Reece informed me.

"So, it's not to get under another woman?" I questioned.

"I can't answer that. You know him better than me," Reece said.

"I thought I did," I muttered as I watched Shane dribble the ball and dunk it to win the game. We stayed outside for a few hours until I got tired. Reece drove me back home, and I soaked in the tub and read a book, trying to distract my mind from thinking about Kamden and Vegas. He probably thought I was taking up with Freddie, which wasn't true. Too much was going on when I woke up in the hospital. I still felt uneasy being in a car sometimes, but I knew it wasn't about the car, but the person who tampered with it to get me out of the race for her own selfish reasons, to win Kamden back. Was I standing in her way? Was Kamden having second thoughts about us? Those were all the things I'd been thinking about for the past few days.

Chapter Twenty-Two

Arianna

A month later, Kamden and I still weren't back together. We were cordial and spoke when I had my first doctor's appointment, but other than that, we hadn't had a conversation about where we stood. I hadn't confronted him about Vegas, and he never offered to tell me what happened. I saw photos of him in the gossip magazine of a woman hanging on his arms and him back racing again. Today, Ralph was pleading guilty to the charges, and I debated about going to the court-house; I didn't want to add to the media circus. I was now going on two months pregnant with a little pouch poking out and eating everything that was placed in front of me. Standing in front of the mirror, looking at my nude body, I saw my curves even more with the added weight gain.

Essence was coming over to take me out to a local restaurant to eat and watch the race. I was over being stuck in the house and beyond ready to move back home since my strength was back. I even had a meeting with Sarai about a few interviews that wanted to talk with me about the crash and what happened. Hearing a knock at the door, I grabbed my robe and slipped it on.

"Come in!"

"You ready?" Essence questioned, twisting the keys around her finger. I walked to my closet and grabbed a pair of jeans and t-shirt with a large hoodie to cover up my stomach. Picking up my Adidas and purse, I lay down on the bed to get into my jeans and slid my socks and shoes on.

"Yep," I told her, standing to grab the brush off my vanity mirror to pull my hair into a ponytail.

"I'm starving," Essence blurted out. I pushed her out of my room, laughing at her dramatics, and turned my light off in my bedroom. We walked out to the living room to see Dad rubbing Mom's feet while watching TV. They looked over at us, and I strolled over to kiss them both on the cheek.

"Heading out to lunch with Essence and then back to my place," I said.

"Are you sure, baby?" Mom asked.

"Yeah, it's time for me to get back to work, and I want to sleep in my own bed."

"Have you talked to Kash?" Dad questioned.

I shook my head no. "Last I talked to him, we had a doctor's appointment."

"Baby, he's not my first choice for you with everything that has happened, but I can tell you he loves you based on the way he was ready to fight your brother in the hospital," Dad told me.

"I hear you, Pops," I said.

"Call us when you head to your place?" Mom requested.

Essence and I waved goodbye as Cicely stepped

inside the house. I hugged her and said I was headed home.

"Where are we heading?" Essence asked.

"I have a taste for burger and fries with a large milkshake."

"The sports bar is popping right now, so we can hang out there," Essence said.

"Did Reece say she was coming?" I asked.

Essence nodded her head, turned the key in the ignition, and reversed out of the driveway.

"She's working at the house today. She said she would try but can't guarantee," Essence explained.

"I need to call Jackson and see what's happening with the charity dinner getting rescheduled," I said.

We were stopped at the light, and my phone vibrated with a new alert of the court details. A picture of Ralph walking into the courthouse with his head down as fans scrambled to get his autograph. I shook my head at the way people behaved when someone was on trial for a crime, yet they still wanted an autograph and picture.

"We're here!" Essence said, and I finally looked up to see us at Dave and Busters. The same place Kamden took me on our first date.

"What are we doing here?" I asked.

"Here to eat. Come on and stop tripping," Essence huffed, grabbed her bag, and stepped out of the car. I rolled my eyes at her antics. I felt she was up to something, but I didn't want to go off on her in public, so I'd wait to see what happened.

She opened the door, and we walked inside. The place was crowded with couples and a few families in the game area.

"How many today?" The hostess asked.

"Two," Essence answered.

"Perfect! Follow me," the hostess said, and we walked behind her toward our booth. She placed us near the bar and the big TV screen to watch the races. I put my purse down, scooted over, and got comfortable, taking the menu out of her hands.

"What can I get you to drink?" she asked.

"I'll take a strawberry milkshake," I said.

"Same," Essence commented.

I flipped the menu over and scanned the burger and fries and dessert menu. I glanced up to see the TV playing the latest race with Kamden coming in fourth place. He jumped out of the car and pushed a crew member to the side after losing. It was typical of him to have an attitude if something didn't go his way. The reporter tried to get a statement from him, and he waved them off.

"You should call him," Essence said.

"Call who?" I retorted.

"Don't play dumb, Ari. Kamden is hurting just as much as you."

"I can't tell." I sipped my milkshake the waitress brought to the table.

"Ready to order?" the waitress asked.

"Can I get the avocado burger with fries and a chocolate chip cookie?" I replied.

"I'll take the lemon wings and fries," Essence told her.

"Be right up," the waitress said and took the menus with her to the back.

I sat back in my seat and continued watching the ESPN commentators' debate about Kamden's loss.

"Do you blame him? Because it was Josie and Ralph?" Essence asked.

"No, I think he believes I blame him, but I'm more pissed that it went on for so long with her trying to push into his life, and I know he said they weren't together."

"But you're worried that maybe he had feelings for her after all?" Essence questioned.

"Is that stupid?"

Essence shook her head no.

"Ari, you're human, Kamden is human. You'll make mistakes, but trust is the most important thing," Essence advised.

"What if I don't trust him?" I asked.

"Then, you don't really love him."

"Maybe we can co-parent the baby?" I mumbled.

"Do you think he'll go for that?" Essence asked.

I chuckled at her statement.

"This is what Kamden was talking about."

"You're right, but I think Kamden would surprise you," Essence stated.

"When did you get on Kamden's team?" I inquired.

"I think he's perfect for you, of course. I didn't think the way you two started out was practical. Kamden has helped you too, with becoming softer," Essence said.

"What about your dating life?" I asked, all about changing the subject.

Essence scratched behind her ear nervously, looking off toward the screen.

"Spill it," I said.

"Nothing to tell. I'm having fun," Essence said.

"I'm happy for you, but who are you having fun with?"

"I'd rather not say."

I gasped in shock.

"I'm your best friend, and you can't tell me?" I pouted, exaggerating.

"In time, I'll tell you. I promise," Essence mentioned, and loud voices caused most of the customers in the restaurant to look over at the front entrance.

I said I was prepared to be in the same room with him beyond the doctor's office, but this was a place I didn't want photographers catching us together and asking questions.

"Oh, look who's here," Essence said and waved Kamden and his friends over as they walked behind the hostess.

I groaned, covering my head with my phone, trying to ignore his hard stare.

Chapter Twenty-Three

Kamden

This was the second time I'd seen her in almost two months, and she looked just as beautiful as the first time the doctor told her she was pregnant after her first checkup. Tripp forced me to come out with him and the guys to have drinks and take my mind off the court case and my breakup with Ari. We barely spoke at the second doctor's visit besides saying hi and bye. It was awkward and forceful, and my mom wanted her to come back over for dinner a few weeks back. I lied and said she wasn't feeling well. Cicely even tried to get me to call and try to make things right with her, but my conscience ate at me about Josie and Ralph causing these problems. I never expected to get her caught up in my shit to the extent that she was almost killed. Maybe love wasn't something I should be given if I ended up hurting the one I loved. One thing I promised her was that I would always be there for our child and not turn out like my father.

"Hey, ladies, what are you doing here?" Tripp

wondered, standing at the end of the booth, staring at Essence.

"Ari was starving, and I wanted to get her out of the house," Essence stated.

"Arianna, are you doing good?" Tripp asked.

She smiled and nodded in answer.

"I'm fine, Tripp, how about you?" she asked.

"Perfect, sorry about the charity race. I told Kamden earlier that day something was weird about Josie and Ralph, but I didn't think it would be something that huge," Tripp confessed, and I grunted, not wanting her to know about them arguing at the racetrack earlier that day. Her eyes expanded wide in shock, and she glared at me.

"Let's go to our table, Tripp," I said.

"You guys can sit with us," Essence mentioned.

"Naw, we have a table over there," I replied.

"Why not? It would be easier," Tripp told me.

"I'm cool with that," Bobby, our other friend, said. He worked for Cyrus Premier Enterprises in the marketing department. We became friends when he worked on the campaign of my first photoshoot years ago.

"See, Bobby's cool with us sitting here," Tripp said as he squeezed into the booth next to Essence.

"Sit next to Ari, Kamden," Essence said sneakily.

Arianna rolled her eyes and moved over, and I sat next to her, trying to keep some distance.

"We have the burger and fries, and wings with fries." The waitress approached the table with their food.

"Thank you," Arianna said as her plate was placed in front of her.

"Gentlemen, what can I get you?" the waitress asked the three of us.

"I'll have the wings like her," Tripp said, and I looked

between him and Essence. She grinned as he picked a fry off her plate. I knew he probably had a crush on her, but I didn't know they were actually dating.

"Anything for you, sir?" Tammy asked.

"Can you bring me a burger and fries, sweetheart?" I asked, and Arianna scoffed and mumbled under her breath.

"Of course, Kash," Tammy stated.

Arianna smacked her lips. "Typical," she said.

"Arianna," Essence said, her tone pleading.

My love was strong and still present as we sat next to each other, and I could feel the pull between us needing to have a conversation.

"What?" Arianna remarked.

"Be nice," Essence fussed.

"Always," Arianna answered by grabbing the ketchup and pouring a little on the side of the plate with her cookie. I watched her break a piece of the cookie off and dip it into the ketchup and pop it into her mouth.

"Arianna, did you really just dump ketchup on your cookie?" Tripp asked.

Arianna pulled back from her sandwich and wiped a piece of the mayonnaise off her lip, and I smirked seeing her eyes grow wide and look around at everyone watching her.

"I'm pregnant," she quipped.

"Kamden, did you know this was the type of food she ate?" Tripp questioned.

I ran a hand down my face and stared at her, wondering how we got so far apart.

"She's pregnant," I repeated.

"He doesn't tell me what to eat; I'm my own person, Tripp. I thought you knew that," Ari advised.

"We all know that, but you two should start talking again. Both of you have been miserable without the other," Tripp said.

"T, leave it alone," I said.

He shrugged and picked up a wing off Essence's plate.

"How was Vegas?" I heard Ari ask.

I looked over at Tripp to signal him to keep his mouth shut. Vegas was still playing in my mind after getting drunk almost every day from the guilt. I wasn't too worried that I would sleep with anyone because Cyrus and Tripp looked after me. We only stayed two days and then flew back home. I put my all into training, working out, and staying with my mom to get away from the paparazzi camped out in front of my home. Every day, they wanted to know how I felt about Josie and Ralph setting Arianna up. I went to visit Ralph one time in jail and almost ended up there myself when I tried to kick his ass. They'd been fucking behind my back for a few months, and she basically talked his dumbass into thinking he could be a big star if I were out of the way. Then Josie noticed Arianna and I getting close, so she manipulated him into thinking Arianna was getting to the top over him.

"Nothing happened," Tripp replied.

"T," I groaned.

"What? You don't want him to tell us all how you've had the biggest orgy in Vegas?" Arianna questioned.

"What are you talking about?" The first time she said something to me besides a hello, she accused me of sleeping with someone else.

"Please, keep it real, Kamden. We all know how you get down in Vegas," Ari spat.

"All we did was drink and gamble," I answered.

"Can you let me out, please? I'm ready to go," she told Essence.

"Arianna, you two should talk and hear him out," Essence said.

"No, thank you," Ari stated.

"You're so stubborn," Essence insisted.

I stood so Ari could get out of the booth, and Essence followed when Tripp jumped up.

"It's fine, Essence," I told her.

"It's the hormones," Essence joked.

Arianna stomped off to the front door, and a swarm of photographers surrounded her. I bolted out of the restaurant to help her.

"Get back! Can't y'all see she's pregnant!" I shouted, grabbing Ari's hand and pulling her to my chest.

"I'm fine, Kamden. Just take me home," she said.

I kissed the top of her head and rubbed her back. Tripp and Bobby walked out of the restaurant with to-go boxes. I forgot about the food I ordered and motioned for Tripp.

"Take Essence home for me," I said.

Ari tried to step out of my hold, and I gripped her tighter around the waist. I escorted her to my car and opened the passenger side door. She slid inside, and I shut the door, stepping over to Tripp.

"I'm taking her home. I'll call you later," I said.

"Yeah, I can see you two need to have a conversation," Tripp said.

"What's up with you and Essence?" I questioned.

"Nothing," Tripp said and grinned, walking backwards to her car. They drove over in my car, and I wasn't going in the direction of his place.

I shook my head and walked around to the driver's side. I shifted in my seat, feeling like it was my first time meeting her. She glowed from the pregnancy, and I wanted to kiss all over her body and rub her stomach, but the way she looked out the window and avoided me, I didn't think we could come back from this. I took off when the light turned green and drove to her house in silence.

Chapter Twenty-Four

Kamden

I pulled up in front of her place forty minutes later. I turned the car off and opened the driver's side door, and she grabbed my hand, stopping me.

"What are you doing?" she questioned me.

"I'm going inside with you," I said.

"I'll be fine."

I sat back in my seat and sighed. She was shutting me out again, same as the hospital.

"Don't shut me out, Ari. We need to talk."

"I haven't shut you out, Kamden. I tell you all the appointments for the baby."

"You know what I mean."

"I'm not doing this with you," she muttered.

"We're doing this, and you're going to listen to me."

"Why? So, you can lie and run off and sleep with someone else?" she spat before she jumped out of the car and slammed the door. I got out of the car, pissed, and chased after her.

"I didn't sleep with anyone in Vegas!" I yelled, following behind her in the building.

"I don't believe you," she snapped and tried to close the door in my face.

"What do I have to do?"

How could I tell her I didn't want her racing anymore? This crash was a wakeup call for me. The guilt I harbored from dealing with Josie and Ralph being jealous of what I had didn't sit well with me. Arianna thinking me to be a manwhore pissed me off; it showed she didn't trust me after all this time. We were building something before everything blew up, and now having to work on getting us back into a place of love would take more than she was probably willing to give. Plus, finding out she was pregnant, I didn't want to add any stress on her and the baby.

"Kash, I need time, okay?" Arianna asked, walking inside the elevator. A few minutes later, we got off in front of her door. She slid the key inside and kicked off her shoes. I took my jacket off and sat on the couch.

"We need to talk."

"I need space."

"How are we going to get through this if we don't talk?" I asked.

"You don't understand," Arianna said.

"What don't I understand?"

"You're the star, Kash! You have everything handed to you, and I'm just getting started," she argued.

"I worked my ass off to get here, Arianna. I won't apologize about that," I spat back.

She threw her hands up in annoyance.

"Right, and now you want me to step aside and put my dreams on hold?" Arianna stated. I ran a hand down my face, thinking about her question.

"Baby..."

Arianna held her hand up to stop me from talking.

"This baby won't stop me from driving, neither will the women you flaunt around town. I suggest you figure out how you're going to deal with both," Arianna informed me, then walked over to the door and held it open. I stared at her to make sure she was seriously acting like I didn't believe in her dreams. Grabbing my jacket, I walked over and stood in front of her face, caressing her cheek.

"This is what I want, Arianna, just you. I can't tell you what the accident did to me; I wanted to kill everyone who had anything to do with hurting you," I explained.

Arianna sighed and looked up into my eyes.

"I just need a little space," Arianna said. I kissed her forehead and walked out of her place and over to my penthouse door. Security would probably call about my car not being parked correctly in the morning, but I'd deal with it later.

* * *

The next morning, I ate the breakfast Cicely made and waited for Sarai to come over to chew me out for the latest news about me. Right as I sipped my coffee, the doorbell rang, and Cicely walked over to open it. Sarai walked inside and came to sit at the counter next to me and dropped her purse and binder.

"Morning," I said.

Sarai clasped her hands together, leaned forward, and watched me out of the corner of my eye.

"Do you like being represented by Lambert Public Relations?" Sarai asked.

"Here we go," I groaned and dropped the newspaper.

180

"No, I'm asking for clarification," Sarai insisted, and Cicely set a plate down in front of her.

"Thanks, Cicely," Sarai said.

"No problem. I'll be in the back, grabbing your laundry," Cicely mentioned, and I nodded.

"Sarai, what did I do this time?"

Sarai opened her binder, pulled out some papers, and tossed them in front of me. I picked them up and noticed they were text messages between Josie and Ralph.

"Where did you get these?" I asked.

"I have my ways," Sarai stated, then she picked up a piece of toast and the strawberry jelly.

I read over the text messages, talking about her trying to do something to my car first, and Josie convinced him to hurt Arianna instead.

Ralph: *I'm tired of that bitch-ass boy thinking he's the man.*

Josie: *Ralph, calm down.*

Ralph: *Why are you sticking up for him?*

Josie: *Baby, I'm with you.*

Ralph: *So, we take him out?*

Josie: *I have an even better plan.*

Ralph: *I want Kash gone.*

Josie: *It's not time.*

Ralph: *Because you're still sleeping with him?*

Josie: *That's ridiculous.*

"Jesus," I huffed out.

"Yeah, and there's a lot more," Sarai said.

"Did you show these to Cyrus?" I questioned.

"He was the one who sent them to me," Sarai said.

"The lawyers need to see this."

"I already sent them over. The problem is that the media got a hold of everything," Sarai explained.

"Which means Arianna will see everything if Josie has texts from me." I realized what Sarai was finally saying.

"Exactly and if she has any compromised pictures or videos..." She trailed her thought, and I immediate caught upon it.

"Fuck!" I shouted.

"Yep," Sarai said.

"Can you send a cease-and-desist letter?" I stood and grabbed my phone to call Arianna.

"I already sent one, waiting for confirmation," Sarai stated, cutting into the pancake.

I dialed Arianna's number, but she didn't pick up.

"Give her some space, Kash. She's newly pregnant and dealing with almost getting killed, and her boyfriend was out with other women," Sarai said.

"It wasn't like that at all. I didn't sleep with those girls," I muttered, taking a seat on the couch and closing my eyes.

"Well, if you would have acted like you had some sense, the perception wouldn't be about you dating other women."

"Anything else, Sarai?" I asked, getting annoyed with her presence. She chuckled and grabbed her purse to head out.

"Don't get mad at me because I tell you about yourself." Sarai came over and tapped me on the forehead.

"You're right."

"I know I am, so get your shit together, and I'll call you later."

"Thanks, Sarai," I said.

"Thank me by giving Arianna a little time," Sarai told me and walked out of my condo. She was right. I needed to focus on work and give Arianna a little space to clear her thoughts, but I didn't want to give her too much time and have her forget what we meant to each other. I grabbed my keys and headed out to talk with Cyrus about the situation and do a few laps on the track. An hour later, I made it to Cyrus Premier Enterprises and parked my car. Getting out, I waved to the security guard and stepped onto the elevator toward Cyrus's office. I stepped off five minutes later, knocked on his door, and heard him call to come inside.

"I was expecting you to come," Cyrus said.

"Sarai just left my place."

"Did you talk with Arianna?" Cyrus questioned.

"Not yet," I said as I flopped down in the chair and kicked my feet up on his desk.

"Reece called and said she wasn't talking to anybody," Cyrus said.

"Sarai said I should give her a little space."

"It didn't help that you went to Vegas," Cyrus chastised and kicked my feet off his desk.

"You know I didn't sleep with anybody, but Arianna's hormones are clouding her judgment," I said.

"You really love her?" Cyrus asked.

"As much as you love Reece. What would you do?"

"Reece and I have a different story, which will be told on a different day. This is about you and Arianna," Cyrus said.

"I barely even sleep now."

"That means you're in love, bro," Cyrus told me.

"Love is too complicated," I said.

"Life is complicated, but when you have love, it can make things a lot easier to handle."

Cyrus muttered and grabbed his phone to make a call.

Chapter Twenty-Five

Kamden

Once I finished talking with Cyrus, I came down to the track to get in a few runs to clear my head. Tripp was standing near the pit watching as I pushed the gas harder and sped up as I reached the right corner. This was the only way to get the stress out of my mind and focus on how to get my girl back. I pulled to the side next to the garage, turned the car off, and jumped out, taking off my helmet.

"How's she handling?" Tripp questioned.

"Good. I might do another lap in a few minutes," I said.

"You talk to Arianna today?" Tripp asked.

"She needs space, so I'm doing what she wants, but if I don't hear from her by tomorrow, I'm busting down her door," I replied, following behind him into the garage.

"Women are something else," Tripp said.

"Yep, and she's pregnant, which makes the guilt even worse."

"Don't blame yourself for Ralph and Josie," Tripp

said as he picked up a towel and wiped the grease off his hands.

"I brought Josie into this mess."

"She knew it wasn't a serious thing with you guys. Hell, I heard she was dating some other reporter at the same time she was dating you," Tripp explained.

"What about Ralph? That's for sure my fault."

"Ralph has always been jealous of you though. It didn't take a rocket scientist to notice all the fake smiles and jokes he tried to brush off," Tripp mentioned.

"I was trying to be cool with him. Even offered to work with him on his driving."

"Which would have caused an even bigger problem," Tripp said.

"Let's change the subject. You want to get something to eat?" I questioned.

"Where do you want to go?" Tripp asked.

I was about to say the shop Cyrus told me about when a text message came in from Arianna that said she was going to a doctor's appointment in a week. I replied okay, closed out my phone, and slipped it in my pocket.

"Are you going to any of the trials?" Tripp asked.

"I doubt it. I hate to make it into a bigger media circus with me being there," I said.

Thirty minutes later, Tripp and I ended up at the sandwich shop that I brought Arianna to and sat in the back corner away from the paparazzi sitting out front, waiting to get a shot of me. Some girls walked up to my table to get an autograph, and at first, I wasn't going to because sometimes they'd end up getting sold to the highest bidder, and I didn't understand why people would want to purchase my autograph that bad. The waitress dropped our sandwiches and drinks down on the table, and we ate while talking about the trial.

"I still can't believe Ralph was that hard up over you guys." Tripp bit into his sandwich and drank from his root beer.

I popped a fry in my mouth and nodded in agreement.

"Same, man. Arianna is pregnant and having my baby," I said, still in shock.

"Do you want a girl or boy?"

"I don't care, as long as the baby is healthy."

"Who are the godparents?" Tripp asked.

Drinking my Sprite, I shrugged my shoulders, not having an answer to the question.

"I haven't thought about that honestly."

"Are you planning on getting a house together?" Tripp questioned.

"Shit, I haven't even thought about that either. Arianna stays in her condo, I have mine. Maybe we should discuss it though."

"Seeing as how you two are bringing a baby in the world, it would help."

"You think, Sherlock?" I jokingly stated.

* * *

After dropping Tripp off at home, I drove over to my mom's place for a few minutes to talk before the day got away from me. She kept texting throughout lunch because she hadn't heard from me all day.

"Finally, the lost son has come home," Mom teased, standing to kiss me on the cheek.

"Sorry, Mom."

"What's going on, son?"

"Nothing much."

"I think you can do better than that, Kamden," Mom said, and turned off her *Planet Earth* program.

"Women."

"Well, I'm the perfect person to give advice," Mom said.

"Arianna is pregnant, Ralph and Josie tried to kill her, and I blame myself."

"That's a lot to handle, son. Have you and Arianna talked about everything?" Mom questioned.

"Not exactly. She needs space right now," I told her.

Mom patted my leg.

"Do you love her?" Mom asked.

"More than anything," I admitted for the first time to my mom.

"Then you give her the space she needs but show her that you trust her and want to build a lasting relationship," Mom said.

"What if I want her to stop driving?" I questioned.

"Would you quit driving?" Mom asked.

"No, I love driving."

"Then don't expect her to quit something she loves. Love is not conditional, Kamden," Mom said.

We stayed up late talking and laughing about old times when I used to get into trouble around the neighborhood, and I ended up falling asleep at her place. The next morning, I had a text from Arianna, and she wanted to talk. I showered and grabbed a few clothes I had left at my mom's place in case I ever needed to change clothes. I ran down the stairs and saw Mom in the kitchen cooking breakfast. I kissed her cheek and told her I'd come by later in the week with Arianna to do lunch or dinner. One day, we'd need to get our families together in person since we were bringing a child into the world together. I jumped in my car, pulled out on the street, and headed to the red light. I turned the radio up, listening to Talk Sports Channel discuss the trial with Ralph.

Chapter Twenty-Six

Arianna

I showered and waited for Kash to come over so we could talk and figure out our next steps. Reece was a big help in figuring out that I couldn't keep putting space between us if my intention all along was to still be with him. It wouldn't be fair to string someone along that tried to make an effort in making our relationship work. At first, I wanted to block him from everything when I saw those text messages and nude pictures of Josie that she sent to him. The girl was obsessed with him, and Ralph was delusional just as much, wanting to kill Kash at first. I knew Cyrus was planning on having a meeting with all his drivers, even going as far as offering therapy if they needed. The doorbell rang, and I hopped up from my chair and checked myself in the mirror with the pair of tights and big t-shirt I wore. Cicely was off today, and I cooked a little food for us to have. I opened the door, and Kamden smiled as I stepped to the side to let him inside. He leaned over and kissed me on the cheek.

"Hey," I said as I closed the door behind him.

"You look beautiful," Kamden said.

"Thanks. Take a seat. Are you hungry?"

"In a minute," Kash said.

"I cooked breakfast if you're hungry, but we can talk first."

"Ari, I want this," he said, pulling me into his chest.

"Me too."

"So, how do we move forward?" Kash asked.

"We need to be honest with each other and no more Vegas unless I'm with you," I muttered as I ran a hand up his chest.

He chuckled and brushed his lips across mine.

"No problem," Kash said.

"Communication and trust are what I ask of you moving forward. Can you handle that?" I asked.

"Of course, Ari," Kash replied.

"What do you want from me?" I asked.

"I need you to stop running away when something gets hard between us. We can only be one if we stand together," Kash explained.

I stuck my hand out for him to shake, and he shook his head, laughing while I giggled, watching the bright smile cross his face.

"I love you, Kash," I said.

"I love you too. But never doubt my feelings about you. You're woman enough for me. Josie wasn't my girl-friend. You're my girlfriend and future wife one day."

"What about me driving?" I questioned.

"I'll always be afraid if you get hurt, but I won't stop you from your dreams," Kash insisted.

"Good, because I planned on training until I couldn't drive anymore."

"I figured," Kash said.

"You get my text about the doctor's appointment next week?" I questioned.

He followed me into the kitchen, and I grabbed a bottle of water out of the fridge, removed the top, and took a sip.

"I did. Is everything okay with you?" Kash asked.

"It's a routine checkup. Nothing serious."

"How does your family feel about the baby?" Kash questioned.

"They were happy. At first, it was shocking, and I thought they'd want to kill you. But my mom talked all the men down in our family, and they're okay with me being pregnant."

"You're really having my baby," Kash whispered, burying his face between my neck and shoulder. I wrapped my arms around his neck, and we stood like that for five minutes before his phone rang. He pulled it out of his pocket, looked at the unknown number, and declined the call.

"That could have been important," I said.

"Everything that's important is right here in front of me," Kash said. I grinned and stood on my tippy toes to kiss his lips.

"I'm headed to the track. You want to go with me?" he asked.

"I can go for a little bit, but I need to talk with Malik about something," I said.

"Everything cool with him?" Kash asked.

"Yeah. He wanted me to stop driving, and I declined, so we came to an agreement," I explained.

"I'll go with you, and then we can stop at the track and do a few laps," Kash said.

I grabbed my purse, slid on my tennis shoes, and

followed Kamden out of my apartment. We headed to his car and went over to meet with Malik before we got heavy into practice.

Twenty minutes later, we parked in my spot, stepped out of the car, and held hands going into Pierce Motors. I saw Jackson and Malik standing at the receptionist desk laughing as Kash and I walked up to them.

"Hey, Arianna," Rachel, the lobby assistant, said.

"Hey, Rachel."

"What are you two doing here?" Jackson asked as he hugged me and shook hands with Kash.

"Malik wanted to talk to me, and I was with Kash, so we came together."

"It wasn't a major thing, princess. I just have an upcoming campaign I'm planning in a few months," Malik said.

"You want to talk in your office?" I asked.

"I'm on my way out to meet with Canon. You coming by for dinner at the house?" he replied.

"Kash, you want to come?" I questioned.

"That's fine," Kash replied.

"Are you cool with this, Malik?" I asked.

"As long as he treats you right, I have no complaints," Malik stated.

"Well, email me the information about the proposal, and we can get together later in the week," I said.

"I will, Ari, and don't forget to take it easy. I had to stop myself from getting you private security," Malik said as he kissed my cheek.

"You overthink too much. Kash and I will be fine," I said.

"She's safe with me, Malik. I promise," Kamden told him.

"I'll hold you to that. She's the only reason I didn't kick your ass over this mess," Malik answered. I rolled my eyes and waved him off as I turned to leave with Kash to head over to watch his practice and maybe get a lap in for myself. Kash closed the door, and I put my seatbelt on and waited for Kash to hop into the driver's side. He reversed out of the parking space, and we headed to Cyrus Premier Enterprises.

Chapter Twenty-Seven

Arianna

Essence and Reece were at the track with Cyrus and Tripp when we pulled up and got out of the car. I hadn't talked to them since I decided to give our relationship another chance, so this would be the first time since the Vegas situation.

"Look at the lovely couple," Essence joked.

"Who are you talking about?" I questioned.

"You and Kamden… duh," Essence said.

"You could have been talking about Reece and Cyrus," I said and stuck my tongue out.

"Is the car ready, T?" Kash asked.

"Yep, you ready to take it for a spin?" Tripp said.

"You already know the answer to that one," Kash said.

"Was it hard learning all this stuff, Tripp?" Essence questioned as she ran a hand up his chest. I lifted my left eyebrow and watched those two flirt constantly, but I didn't think they were serious.

"Nope, you should let me teach you how to ride," Tripp said, flirting back with Essence.

"Okay, you two. Cool off please. Tripp, can I get a lap in as well?" I asked.

"You sure, Arianna?" Tripp challenged.

"Yep, I won't be driving fast. I just want to get behind the wheel to keep my skills fresh," I said.

Kash and Tripp walked off, and I watched as they got into his car together to take a spin around the track. I would wait and go after him since this wasn't my normal track to drive on, but Cyrus was okay with me hanging around when I needed to get in practice.

"How did Kash get started in driving?" Essence asked me.

"He used to get in trouble with stealing cars and hanging with bad crowds."

"His mom got him into All Hands Homes and hanging with the kids at center. I met him right after," Cyrus said.

"Maybe I need to learn how to race so I can meet a man," Essence commented.

All of us laughed at her outburst and watched as Kash drove off to do a lap around the track. An hour later, I was in the car, preparing to pull in next to the pit.

"How did she feel?" Tripp asked me.

"The cones helped, but I want to work on doing sling-shots," I said.

"I think before you fully show and can't drive anymore, we can make this happen," Tripp said. I nodded in response, getting out of the car and walking toward Kash and Reece.

"What do you think, Cyrus?" I asked, motioning toward the car.

"You're good, Arianna, never doubt that. This sport needs you, and I'm proud to call you a friend," Cyrus said.

"So that means I can go up against you next time?" I asked.

"Keep working on your groove, and we'll see what happens," Cyrus said.

Kash stood behind me, hugging me to his chest, and we talked with everyone before it got too late, then headed over to my family's house to have dinner.

* * *

My niece Madison ran around the table as Eddison Jr. chased after her. I laughed at her trying to hide under my dad to avoid getting caught.

"You're going to have to deal with this once you have your baby, Arianna," Mom said.

"Are you excited for another grandbaby?" I asked.

"I already have plans to add another room in the house," Mom said.

"This place is going to turn into a nursery," I said.

"Kamden, how are you feeling about the pregnancy?" Dad asked.

"At first, I was shocked, but I'm happy about becoming a father," Kash replied.

"I like to hear that," Dad said.

"What's up, family?" Malik asked as he walked inside, kissed, and hugged my niece and nephew, and Mom. He shook hands with Dad and brother. Gabriella was in the kitchen finishing up the catfish dend baked potatoes. It was a huge spread laid out for us to enjoy. I rubbed the back of Kash's head, while his hand caressed my thigh.

"Hey, Uncle Malik!" Madison said.

"Madison, are you causing problems, princess?" Malik asked.

"Never," Madison spoke, raising her hands to be picked up.

"I'm starving," I said.

"When is your appointment?" Mom asked.

"It's coming up in a week," I said.

"Keep us updated, Ari. I know you're grown, but you're still our baby," Mom told me.

"I promise," I said.

"Dinner is ready!" Gabriella said.

"Finally."

"Stop being grumpy," Kamden said, kissing my cheek.

I grinned and kissed his lips as Malik and Dad groaned at the PDA we showcased, and we started eating right away. Two hours later, we ended up at his place, lying in bed, watching a movie with the covers wrapped around us. I lay in his arms until I fell asleep.

* * *

A week later, I was in the mall, walking around with Reece, Essence, and Sarai, picking up a few things for the baby even though I wasn't really showing.

"This is cute." Essence held up a onesie that said, 'My Auntie is the Best.'

"I wonder why?" I chuckled.

"I need to be prepared for my godchild," Essence said.

"Have you guys decided where you'll live?" Reece asked.

"No, we've been so wrapped up in work, moving hasn't come into my mind."

"Arianna, did you see this crib?" Sarai mentioned, standing near the furniture section.

"It's cute, but I want something a little more tradition-al," I said.

"I'll keep looking. I talked to Kash about the text messages," Sarai commented.

"We talk about everything now. Going forward with no secrets," I said.

"Glad to hear that," Sarai said.

"Check this diaper bin out, Ari!" Reece called out.

"I'm really going to be somebody's mom," I muttered to myself.

"Which means your life is no longer your own, boo," Essence announced.

Essence's comment reminded me that I had to come to terms with knowing that my decisions had to include Kash and our future child going forward. Racing was my dream, but it wasn't the only thing to Arianna Pierce now that she was a mother-to-be and a girlfriend. We stayed in the mall for another hour before going out to lunch then dropping me off at home where I rested up after a long day of being on my feet.

Chapter Twenty-Eight

Kamden

I moved my hand under her dress to skim her hips and thighs. Arianna breathed lightly at my touch, while I explored the soft lines from her pregnancy progressing. Our breakup enlightened me to know that putting things off and not being honest with myself and the one I love could cause miscommunication. Relationships were still new to me and having the responsibility of not one, but two people looking toward me to put their needs ahead of mine, had caused me to grow up faster than I ever imagined. To see the unconditional love in her eyes as we both knew this was forever, and we would never be separated again. Our past mistakes wouldn't define the future we would build together. Arianna bent down and captured my face with both hands parting my lips as I removed her thong. She knew wearing a thin piece of cloth would push me over the edge, and I groaned feeling how wet she was for me.

"Kash..." Arianna whispered as she planted her hands on my shoulders.

Her smell was intoxicating as she straddled my lap.

We'd finished dinner, and I wanted her for dessert and couldn't wait to get upstairs. Since the movers showed up earlier today with our new furniture, we'd been off and on organizing everything to make it a home for our family.

"Kash isn't here right now," I replied.

I pressed my palms against her round ass, helped to lift her up on the table, and maneuvered my chair to face her. As I lifted my shirt over my head, Arianna removed her sweater dress, palming her six-month, rounded tummy. I ran my hand across, feeling the baby kick, and I grinned before leaning over to kiss her lips.

"I love you," Arianna said, spreading her legs wider.

"I love you, and I'm sorry for all the hurt and pain. I was stupid for not listening to you about Ralph and Josie."

"Show me how sorry you are instead of telling me."

Squeezing her thigh, I stepped out of her hold and grabbed a pillow from the couch to make sure she was comfortable. Putting it behind her back, I scooted the chair up close and dipped my tongue in her sweet pussy.

"Ahhh... Yesss... Kamden."

As my hands roamed intimately over her breasts, she gasped. I squeezed her right then left breast. Arianna still had a few bruises from the accident on her inner thigh, and I kissed each one, knowing I'd never forgive myself for putting her in harm's way. I would work extra hard to let her know she'd be protected from here on out, as the love of my life, best friend, and mother of my child.

"Mmmmm... baby, your taste is so sweet."

The softness of her curves even before she was pregnant had only enhanced, and the need to always touch her when we were near probably made me seem obsessed.

"You remember the first time you ate my pussy?"

Arianna questioned, and I nodded, closing my eyes as I teased her clit with my tongue.

I kissed up her thigh, then her stomach, pulling her breasts out of each cup. "Today and the rest of our lives is all about you, baby."

"Ughh... Kash!" she cried out. I found out her nipples were sensitive from being pregnant.

"Shhh... I got you, baby," I responded, teasing her clit with simultaneous pleasure. Her dark nipples stood erect as she'd gone up a cup size from when we met the first time.

"Please, I need you," Arianna moaned, wrapping her leg around my waist.

"Unbuckle my pants and take what's yours, baby," I demanded, exploring each blemish she cried about from stretch marks to swelling. I placed kisses all over as she panted in anticipation.

Undoing my pants, Arianna eased my dick out of my boxers as she taunted me with her fingers, rubbing up to the mushroom tip. Her other hand caressed the hairs at my base, and my head dipped back in pleasure. Closing my eyes, I grunted, not ready to come so quickly.

"Stop teasing me," I muttered.

Arianna ran her thumb over the tip of my dick as precum jolted out and stuck it in her mouth. That was all it took for me to grip her chin, lock eyes with her, and slide into her warm sex. A wave of ecstasy throbbed through me knowing this was home.

"Fuck... Arianna," I hissed, pulling out then thrusting back inside.

She breathed in deep, soul-drenching drafts. I didn't want to fully be chest to chest, so I decided to find a different solution. I picked her up, and she automatically wrapped her arms around my neck. I walked us to the couch and sat with her straddling me. I fully succumbed to her welcoming body. Her body melted against mine, and we found the tempo that bound our bodies together. Arianna buried her face in my neck; the feeling was much more than sexual desire. This wasn't just sex; it was making love.

"Damn... Arianna!" I moaned involuntarily. No woman had ever had this type of pull over me. An electric shock scorched through her body as we both came at the same time. I released in her womb, feeling exhausted and ready for bed. She kissed my cheek as she slipped in and out of consciousness.

"Baby," Arianna muttered.

"Huh," I mumbled.

Arianna giggled at me.

"Are you falling asleep?"

"No," I replied, knowing I was lying.

"We have a doctor's appointment in a few minutes, so we need to get cleaned up," Arianna reminded me, and I yawned, wrapping my arms around her waist.

"I know. I just need a few minutes to rest my eyes, baby."

"We need to shower, Kamden, and the clinic is all the way across town."

"Okay, but it's your fault for having control over my dick."

"How do I have control over it?" she questioned, sliding out of my arms, and standing, extending her hand toward me.

"Because you made my dick submit. Now that you're pregnant, it's even worse. It never wants to leave you alone. So, blame yourself, sexy," I said as I lifted her palm, kissing the back of her hand.

"We ruined each other," she replied, kissing me on the lips. Leaving the trail of clothes behind, we headed up to the master bedroom to shower and change.

* * *

An hour later, we pulled up to the doctor's office, and I helped her out of the car. I didn't mention the surprise, but her parents knew. They helped to organize everything because she was good at snooping around, so I had everything sent to them. I felt my phone vibrate as I walked in behind Arianna so she could sign in and saw a message from Ree.

Ree: *Hey, we're all set!*
Me: *Thanks, Ree.*
Ree: *Anytime, and she's going to love it.*
Me: *Thanks again.*

The engagement ring was handcrafted with our initials and the date we met. Reece helped me plan the dinner with our close friends and family.

The nurse called us back to the room. Arianna grabbed the gown from the nurse to change, and I helped her remove her top, then shorts.

"I can't wait to find out what we're having," Arianna said.

"What do you think about waiting for the birth instead?"

"You want to be surprised?" Arianna asked, leaning back on the bed as the doctor knocked, announcing herself.

"I think it'll be good to wait so nothing leaks out," I told her.

Arianna nodded in agreement.

"Hello, parents to be," Doctor Joy said.

"Hey, Joy," Arianna replied.

"Today, we have a routine checkup. Did you two want to know what you're having?" Doctor Joy asked.

Both of us shook our heads. Pulling out her chart, she discussed Arianna's measurements since the last visit and checked the heartbeat from the ultrasound.

"You're progressing along well, Arianna. You're six months today, and both Mommy and baby are healthy. Continue to take it easy for me and make your next appointment in six weeks," Doctor Joy stated.

"She will, Doc," I told her, rubbing her stomach.

Doctor Joy patted my shoulder and walked out so Arianna could get redressed.

Forty-five minutes later, we were driving to her parents' house, and she noticed a few cars in the driveway.

Arianna looked out the window and groaned. I turned the car off, pulling the key out, and opened the door to help her out since my truck was high up, towering over every other car.

"You men and your cars," she commented.

"What's that supposed to mean?" I questioned, stretching my arm over her shoulder and pulling her into me.

"It means we need a family car once the baby gets here," Arianna said and knocked on the front door.

"Whatever you want, baby," I answered as the doorknob turned, and her brother and nephew stood at the door.

"Look what the cat dragged in. Little sis, you're getting big," Eddison Jr. joked and shook my hand. Arianna pushed him on the shoulder and picked up her nephew, giving him a kiss.

"Where's the rest of the family?" Arianna questioned.

"Out back, cooking and waiting for you."

"Who's all over here? I saw about ten cars out front," Arianna asked, heading to the backyard.

"Go see for yourself," Eddison responded, and she glared.

"Ugh, fine."

"Are you sure you can deal with her spoiled ass?" Eddison asked.

"Wouldn't change anything about her," I told him, following behind her, waiting to hear her reaction.

"Ahhh!!" Arianna screamed.

I smiled and caught up with her taking in the decorations. Reece planned everything over the past few weeks. Even though Arianna and I separated for a short while, I knew I wanted her to be my wife, so I put everything in place for this day to happen. It was an engagement party and a family get together all in one. My mom was here with my extended family and friends. The banner read *Will You Marry Me, Arianna?* I had everyone holding up the words while Reece came over and slipped the ring in my hand. Arianna stood with tears in her eyes, and I dropped to my knee as she grabbed my hand. Opening the box, she gasped in shock. It was a white diamond with our birth colors blended on the top, shaped like a heart.

"Arianna Pierce, I love you, and I've never felt whole until you walked into my life. We met under circumstances that normally people would think was a joke and not sustainable for a lasting love. But I promise you, baby,

I'll do everything in my power to make you happy for the rest of your life if you give me a chance," I said, waiting for an answer.

Arianna looked up at her family, specifically at Malik, and he smiled, winking at her, and she smiled back.

"Yes. I'll marry you, Kash," Arianna muttered, letting me slide the ring on her finger. I knew I would need Malik's blessing for her to feel comfortable with moving forward as a family as close as they were, constantly fighting like cats and dogs. Malik was her protector, and now I was stepping into that role.

"Congrats!" Everyone screamed, and I stood and pressed my lips to hers, wanting to succumb to the tender touch of her hands. We didn't have time for a quickie in her parents' house, so I had to think of something else to get my dick to go down.

"I guess he's ready for round two," Arianna teased as she pulled back, wiping the lipstick off my mouth.

I lifted her hand, kissing her palm again, as her mother and Essence came over, pulling her out of my hold.

"Get used to it, bro. Welcome to the family again, man," Malik said, slapping hands with me.

"Thanks, man," I replied.

The music was turned up, and I talked with her brothers, watching her laugh and joke with our parents.

"I heard you're thinking of retiring?" Eddison questioned.

It was in the back of my mind to spend more time with my family, and now that I was coming up on twenty-six, I didn't want to spend the rest of my life not being there for the special moments. Cyrus helped me in investing to diversify, so money wasn't an issue. Getting into other ventures was a possibility, maybe even owning a racing team.

"Not sure yet. All depends on where Arianna's head is at," I stated, taking a sip of my beer.

"Once the baby comes, you'll figure it out. Enjoy these moments."

Chapter Twenty-Nine

Arianna

My mom hugged and passed me a plate of food with ribs, corn on the cob, baked beans, and corn bread with a glass of lemonade. Cicely ran behind Madison, and Major was up under his dad. This was truly a surprise I didn't see coming at all, and I was grateful to know that so many people loved us and wanted to see us win.

"How shocked are you?" Essence asked.

"Extremely shocked. Did you know about this?" I waved around at the decorations.

"Reece told me about it when you came home from the hospital. During the time you and Kash weren't talking, he was still thinking about you," Essence stated.

"Am I too young to have a baby and get married?" I questioned aloud.

"We can't answer that for you, Arianna. Besides, your father and I got married when we were young, and I never once regretted my choices. Kash loves you and despite his crazy ex and his teammate, you two belong together," Mom said.

"She's right. Since we've been talking, Kash hasn't stopped looking over here at you, girl," Essence commented.

"Reece, did you help pick the ring?" I asked, twisting the ring back and forth on my finger.

"He designed the ring. I just picked it up and set up the decorations," Reece replied.

I ran a hand across my belly; this baby was sitting on my bladder.

"What are your plans after having the baby?" Mom inquired.

Thinking about my career and being in a high-profile relationship, I wasn't sure how to approach the conversation with Kamden about returning to racing again. I knew our parents and Cicely would help watch the baby when it was born. Plus, after talking with a therapist, the nightmares had slowly faded away.

"I want to start driving again."

Cicely brought Madison over from the pool, and she reached out to me, wanting to sit in my lap.

"Hey, Maddie poo," I said, kissing her cheek.

She giggled, hiding her face in my chest.

"How does Kash feel about you racing again?" Essence queried.

"He was pissed at first, but we talked about everything, and he supports me."

"I don't blame him. You're the most important person to him. Communication is important, Arianna," Cicely stated, picking up her cup and taking a sip of lemonade. Glancing over at the guys standing around talking, I held a hand over my eyes to block out the sun. Kash caught me staring, and he winked back at me. A flutter in my heart caused me to blush at the simple things he did to make me realize he was it for me. To think if I had not have taken that trip to Vegas and been impulsive, then things could have turned out differently for me.

"Have you talked with Sarai?" Reece interrupted the silence.

"No. Lately, she's been working a lot for CC."

"I think she's going through another breakup. She might need us to check in on her tomorrow," Reece said, passing a piece of cupcake to Maddie.

If I had a daughter, I hope she turned out like my niece. She was so smart even at four. Between her and my nephew, I couldn't believe how they reminded me of Malik and myself. I knew Kamden probably thought I would say no when he proposed, but after the fight with my brother in the hospital, I was disappointed in them for stepping so out of character. I didn't blame Kash for the actions of his old teammate or Josie anymore. The therapist helped me to see that individual responsibility came into question, and he'd made it clear many times they weren't a couple. Now, I was about to be the wife of Kamden 'Kash' Coleman and the mother of his child.

"We should do a girl's night in or something," I answered, feeling a presence behind me. I looked up and saw Kash taking a seat next to me before he grabbed Maddie out of my arms. She was more in love with Kash than her own dad.

"Hey, Maddie Poo," Kash said, tickling her stomach. Maddie burst into laughter, and she tried to tickle him back.

"Kash, are you ready to handle a daughter like Arianna?" Essence teased.

"The question is if she can handle me as her father.

She's not allowed to date until she's forty," Kash said, and we all laughed at his statement.

"How can you say she's not allowed to date until then when we hooked up when we were both in our twenties?" I fussed, crossing my arms over my chest.

Cicely and my mom stood, ready to leave the table; they knew how I could get with my attitude.

"Babe, I'm kidding. She can date at thirty," Kamden replied as he entwined our hands.

"So that means I shouldn't have sex anymore until I'm thirty, right?" I hinted, and the reaction on his face made me chuckle.

"Now she got your attention," Essence told him.

"Maddie Poo, you see how your auntie hurt my feelings," Kamden said, getting my niece on his side.

"She can't save you now, baby," I said, running a hand up his arm.

Reece and Essence laughed, and we continued talking and joking together as Maddie started getting hungry by calling out for food. My brother came over and picked her up. The afternoon was fun with friends and family coming in and out, congratulating us on our engagement and new house.

* * *

I left Kash at home to put the rest of the house together and came to meet up with Jackson and Malik at Pierce Motors to talk about me driving again.

"Hi, Jackson," I sweetly said as he stood, walked around his desk, and pulled me in a hug before I sat in a chair.

"What are you doing here, pregnant lady?" Jackson asked, rubbing my belly.

"Malik, what are you doing here? I thought you had a meeting in Seattle?" I questioned.

"It was postponed. I have too much to catch up on here. How is uncle's little baby doing?" Malik asked, standing, and coming toward me. He bent down and kissed me on the forehead and rubbed my belly. Surprisingly, he'd been the most responsive candidate to my pregnancy and the most helpful in my family. If Kash couldn't take me to my doctor's appointment, Malik or my mom took me.

"It's doing well."

"So, what's up with you?" Malik asked.

I cleared my throat and sat up straight, staring right into Jackson's eyes.

"Are you sure about this?" Jackson inquired, already knowing what I was asking.

"Yes."

"What am I missing?" Malik asked.

"She wants to get back out there and drive," Jackson told him.

"Ugh, really, Ari. Don't you need to retire or something?" Malik asked.

"Why would I retire?" I asked.

He motioned at my belly, and I laughed.

"I'm pregnant. It only lasts nine months," I said.

"But don't you want to stay at home? What about Kash?"

"It's my decision, Malik. I'm not saying I want to drive tomorrow. Once I give birth, maybe a year after the baby is born."

Malik blew out a breath of frustration.

"I promise I'm fine. Don't worry." I grasped his hand, while he stood next to me.

"Give it a year or two and see how you feel afterwards. Once the babies come into the picture, you might change your mind," Jackson said.

"Did Emery change her mind about working after JJ was born?" I questioned.

"Good point," Jackson said and chuckled.

A knock on the door interrupted us.

"Come in," Jackson called out.

"Hey, baby." Emery smiled as she swayed inside the room and looked over me.

"Emery! Perfect timing," I said.

"Hey, Arianna. You look cute, boo," Emery said.

"Can you say hello to your husband first?" Jackson grumbled, causing us both to laugh.

Emery let me go and walked around his desk, standing on her tippy toes to kiss him on the lips. She slid her arms around his neck.

"We don't want to see you two making out. Take that somewhere else," Malik joked.

"Sorry, what are you doing here, Emery?" Jackson asked, clearing his throat while keeping his arm around her waist.

"I wanted to take you to lunch if you're not busy," Emery said.

Jackson checked his watch then lifted his eyes to Malik and me.

"I'm good," I said.

"Me too. You two crazy kids go ahead," Malik said.

They chuckled as Malik and I walked out of his office.

"Where are you headed now?" Malik wondered, hitting the button for the elevator.

"To hang with my fiancé," I teased, showing off my ring.

"I am happy for you, sis. I only want the best for you," Malik told me.

"I know, and I want the best for you as well, so stop playing around and settle down," I told him, pointing my finger at his chest.

"Don't put that voodoo on me. I'm good being single," Malik replied.

The elevator doors opened, and I stepped off, rubbing my small belly. I waved bye to Malik as the doors closed.

"Hey, baby," I said, answering the call through my Bluetooth speaker.

"What are you doing?" Kash asked.

"Driving home," I said.

"Good, we can talk then?" Kamden said.

"What's up?" I replied.

"I'll tell you when you get here," Kamden said.

I turned off the freeway, pushing the gas a little more. My gut told me something was wrong and if Kash was in trouble, I would curse him out first and then call the lawyer. It didn't take too long for me to get on our street and hit the gate to drive inside and park. I shut the car off and stepped out. I put my key in the front door and heard it chirp as I called out Kash's name.

"Where are you?" I asked.

"In the kitchen," Kamden said.

I turned the corner and spotted Kamden at the fridge, grabbing a bottle of water. I put my purse on top of the counter and walked over to wrap my arms around his waist.

"Tell me what's wrong," I said.

He grinned and kissed me on the tip of my nose.

"Sarai called and said the *Daily Morning Show* wants to do an interview with us," Kamden said.

I lifted my right eyebrow. "Why?"

"With the crash and our whirlwind romance, they wanted to get an exclusive interview. Sarai told them no, but they emailed again once they heard about our engagement," Kamden said.

"Nope. They've been more than vile with their reporting. I'd rather not."

"That's fine. She has an interview request with a sports magazine too," Kamden stated.

"That could be fun."

"I missed you today."

"Show me how much," I taunted, stepping out of his embrace, and sashaying out of the kitchen. He followed and smacked me on the ass, I giggled and tried to get out of his hold as we kissed in the hallway, ripping each other's clothes off. Kamden picked me up bridal style and walked me to the living room and laid me down. We made love in every room of the house for the rest of the day.

Chapter Thirty

Arianna

A month later

"Jonathan, can you add a little more lip gloss to Arianna?" Sarai asked. After declining the interview with the *Daily Morning Show*, we agreed to a photoshoot and an interview about our relationship and careers. I was standing in front of Kash wearing only a thong with my breasts covered by Kash's arm. At first, he wasn't going for it, but after a little convincing with me agreeing to a quickie in the dressing room, he was fine with it as long as it came out tasteful, and we had full control of the final shots.

"You look great, guys," Sarai said.

"She looks beautiful; I'm just here dressed," Kamden joked.

"Ohh, poor baby," I teased.

"Kamden, look down at Arianna with one arm on her stomach and the other covering her breasts," the photographer called out as Jonathan finished putting a coat of clear lip gloss on my lips.

"Arianna, keep your head forward," the photographer

instructed, snapping another shot. He then walked up a little closer for the next shot.

"Okay, we can take a thirty-minute break so you can do the interview and eat," the *Sports Racer* reporter announced.

"That works," Sarai stated.

"You two can take a seat over there," the reporter said, pointing near the chairs under the lights. They had us at Milk Studios in Los Angeles. They were well known for film, TV, and magazine shoots.

"Thanks again for meeting with us, Arianna. We already spoke with Sarai and understand certain things will be off limits," Chanelle said, turning the recorder on.

Kamden helped me over to the chair to sit.

"I missed you today," Kamden told me.

He gripped my chin, pecked my lips twice, and I wiped the lipstick off his lips.

"I missed you too, Kash," I teased, calling him by his nickname. Chanelle sat across from us and smiled, pointing the recorder closer to us on the table. An assistant brought over two cups of water.

"Thank you," I said.

"So, let's start from the beginning. How did you two meet?" Chanelle asked.

Kamden and I peered at each other and grinned.

"Do you want the Vegas story or the story of us dating officially?" I inquired.

"I heard the Vegas story was a one-night stand. Is that true?" Chanelle challenged.

"It was," I answered.

"Did you expect to end up together after a one-night stand?" Chanelle wondered.

"I didn't like him at first; he was too cocky for me.

Besides, I'm a little cocky, so two strong personalities coming together wasn't my ideal mate," I said, grasping Kamden's hand.

"This wasn't the typical romance I take it?" Chanelle questioned.

"It wasn't, but I'm happy to have her in my life," Kamden told her.

"See? He can be sweet sometimes," I joked.

Kamden laughed, and Chanelle continued taking notes in her booklet. We continued answering questions and taking photos for the rest of the afternoon. Around six that evening, we changed and made it to the annual sports awards for the celebration of athletes in all fields. Kamden was nominated for Athlete of the Year, and this was our official debut on the red carpet as a couple. Sarai was walking us down the press line as the flashbulbs went off when I heard my name called to pose for the camera. Kamden kissed the side of my forehead and squeezed my waist. I smiled and looked up into his eyes.

"Arianna to the left, Arianna to the left!" the photographers yelled.

Sarai pointed over to us to come forward for an interview with *Daily Morning Show*.

"If you're tired, let me know, and I'll take you home, babe," Kamden said.

"I'm good."

"Arianna, you look so beautiful. How's the pregnancy going?" Linda asked, pointing the mic toward me.

"Thank you, Linda. Everything is going well," I answered.

"When can we expect you two to come on the show?" Linda asked.

"Kash! Kash, can we get a picture!" a second photographer asked from ABH network.

"Talk with Sarai. She handles all our interviews," I told Linda before I took Kamden's hand to take more photos.

We finished taking pictures and stepped inside the venue. As some of the drivers came up to us, I noticed Tripp with Essence on his arm. My mouth hung open in shock. He cleaned up nicely in a black tuxedo, and his hair pulled in a tight bun. They even matched with her wearing a long, black dress with a slit on the side and a gold clutch and necklace.

"What are you doing here, Essence?" I asked.

"Hey, Kash. I came as Tripp's date," Essence said, rubbing up his arm.

"Are you two dating?" I questioned as Kamden and Tripp shook hands.

"We're friends," Essence replied.

Tripp didn't like the answer to her question based on his facial expression. He whispered in her ear, and she giggled, standing on her tippy toes, and kissed his lips.

"Ari, stay out of it please," Kamden said.

"Did you know about this?" I asked, turning toward him.

He ran a hand through his hair and sighed.

"Not my business," Kamden answered as he kissed me on the lips.

"Well, it's my business if it has to do with my bestie," I said.

"Have you seen Cyrus and Reece?" Kamden asked.

"Yeah, they're inside talking," Tripp told him.

"Let's grab our seats," I stated and walked inside, bypassing the security line.

The room was full of people from agents, publicists, crew, celebrities, and athletes. I noticed Cyrus and Reece laughing together, and I strolled over with Kamden following behind. I reached over and hugged them.

"You guys look amazing, Ari!" Reece said.

"Thank you. Cyrus, how are you?" I asked.

"I'm good, Arianna. I heard you guys did a great job on your photoshoot earlier," Cyrus said.

"It was good. Exhausting but good."

"Get used to it; it's only the beginning," Reece said.

"Kamden, did you prepare a speech for tonight?" Reece asked.

"Nope. I don't do these things, but Sarai forced me to make an appearance," Kamden told her.

"At least your award is up first," I said.

"That's true, and then you two can leave if you want. I plan on leaving," Cyrus said.

"I like that idea," Kamden replied.

"Can we have everyone please take their seats?" The announcer stated. This event mirrored the award shows with an intimate field of tables with drinks and food with a small stage up front. The decorations of red, white, and black across the room with USA flags and team colors for each section. I saw cameras from every network filming. We clapped as Jagger Spicer from the Atlanta Lions basketball team stepped up to the mic and pulled out a card to read the first award.

"Our first award up for the night is for a dynamic gentleman that has made a huge impact on the industry, and he's known as the bad boy of the racing world. Which is hard to do when you have Cyrus Davidson sitting next to you," Jagger joked, and the entire room laughed at his comment.

"Kash is a longtime friend of mine, so I can rag on him. So, without further ado, Kash, come up here and grab this award," Jagger advised, and everyone stood while I jumped up and kissed Kamden on the lips as he pulled me into a tight hug. I watched him trod over to the stage and grab the award out of Jagger's hand.

"Wow! Are you guys sure about this? Thanks, Jagger, and to the entire team here and all my friends. The one thing I can say above all is that I'm grateful for the opportunity to do what I love and appreciate being able to fall asleep and wake up next to the most important person in my life who brings me nothing but happiness. Ari, you're my queen, and I can't wait to marry you and bring our little one into the world," Kamden spoke, and I wiped the tears from my eyes. My life had changed for the better, and I knew it was because I took a chance and didn't let my dreams fall through the cracks. I met someone who celebrated the good and bad parts of me.

"I love you," I mouthed to Kamden.

Epilogue

Kamden

One year later

It was finally time for Arianna to get back into competition since her crash. We were all dressed in our white shirts that read Arianna's car number on the front and the Coleman name on the back. We'd eloped to Vegas where we met and got married with close friends and family along with little baby Kash by our side. I hadn't gone back to race in over a year and a half, and was taking time to raise Kash, and make sure Arianna was back to one hundred percent. Josie was still in prison for attempted murder after Ralph confessed that she manipulated him. She thought Arianna was getting in the way of being more high profile on the racing circuit. After the drama with her family not trusting me, it took a while to have them on board with us getting married. Arianna wanted a big wedding, so we planned on doing a bigger one later this year since she was pregnant for our Vegas trip. I was more in love with her than ever before and wanted another baby, but she'd just gotten comfortable with her size after the birth of

Kash. So, we decided to wait and try in another two years, after she'd put in more time driving. She was no longer working for Pierce Motors or Cyrus Premier Enterprises with setting up charity events. She was solely focused on driving and building her career. Sarai had her giving interviews and doing photoshoots. She was plastered on every magazine cover. We even did a couple's interview for *Race Inc.* magazine with little Kash.

"Let's go, Ari!" I heard Eddison Jr. call out. Arianna turned, looking up from the ongoing interview to smile and wave at him. Little Kash clapped his hands together, and I kissed his cheek.

"You see Mommy? Huh?" I asked my son.

He giggled and squirmed, wanting to get down and run toward her. The interview ended, and the drivers prepared to ride. The drivers revved their engines and a few seconds later, they all took off. She was right behind Daniel Wallace, one of the second-highest paid drivers in the league. Reece reached over to grab little Kash out of my arms as Cyrus had his arm around her shoulders.

"She's doing good. Brody has been working with her a lot," Cyrus said.

"He told me," I replied.

"Are you still planning on having a big wedding?" Cyrus asked.

"If that's what she wants, I'll make it happen," I answered, whistling as she did another lap, still behind Daniel.

"I didn't expect to see you both married. I'm happy for both of you," Reece spoke.

The entire track erupted in applause as Ari came from behind and won the race. I hugged Reece and walked out to the track, meeting Arianna halfway as she ran into my arms.

"Thanks, Ree," I answered.

"Baby, I did it!" Ari screamed and grasped my face, kissing me on the lips. I lifted her up, and she wrapped her legs around my waist as our family and friends surrounded us.

"I love you, Ari," I said.

"I love you more, Kamden," Arianna said, and we hugged each other as little Kash called out for his momma.

* * *

I hope you enjoyed Arianna and Kash's story. Check the sneak peek of "**Pressure**" on the https://books2read.com/u/bPeDqr next page. If you love romantic comedy, fake relationships, enemies to lovers, find it here, "**Something Gained**." Click the link here https://books2read.com/u/baGLYy. My stories of friends finding love started with the Heart of Stone series that includes a host of characters and family. "**Broken**" book 1 Emery and Jackson a sports, one night stand, workplace romance is here: https://books2read.com/u/3LoelX

Then you can continue with a fun side story of Emery and Jackson with "**Valentine's Day** short here: https://books2read.com/u/4jAypY

Jordan, her best friend's story, continues here in "**Rebirth**" book 2 a single dad, widow billionaire romance here: https://books2read.com/u/ba2OMx

* * *

Please also check out a second-chance workplace romance here, **"Renew Book 4"** https://books2read.com/u/4NXyPG with a host of characters intertwined.

Follow Desiree and Gabriel in **"Temptation"** a standalone contemporary, sports, curvy girl romance. Check it out here https://books2read.com/u/mle1Vv

Check out dark mafia romance here that started my journey with Antonio and Sabrina in **"Ruthless Book 1"** https://books2read.com/u/4AxKLo

The relationship continues in **"Savage"** book 2 as they get to know each other and their families: https://books2read.com/u/bpED6g

Antonio and Sabrina have more work to do in **"Beast"** book 3 right here: https://books2read.com/links/ubl/4AxKOd

* * *

Did you know Janice and Carlo have a book? Well grab this dark mafia romance with emotional scars, and betrayal right here: https://books2read.com/u/b6je6M

Any fans of forbidden romance, political? Check out **"Mutual Agreement"** https://books2read.com/u/mgzzWX a steamy romance. Download the full novel of **"Nasir"** click the link here.

Have you checked out **"She's All I Need"** click here https://books2read.com/u/49lkeW a sports, opposites attract romance. What about dark romance that has everything from steamy romance, opposites attract, suspense, thriller, celebrity, and more **"Stolen Book 1"** https://books2read.com/u/mvZlgV Don't miss the follow up Joaquin and Sofia's story in book 2 **"Saved"** https://books2read.com/u/4DWwLd

The conclusion for Joaquin and Sofia comes full circle in **"Betrayed"** here: https://books2read.com/u/4A5LGp

***

Catch up with favorite characters in this holiday short romance which includes spoilers. "Holiday collection" here https://books2read.com/u/bzd59G

For small town, single mom stories check out "Until Serena" https://books2read.com/u/mej8vr.

All curvy girl, plus size romance lovers get into **"I Deserve His Love"** a standalone, second chance romance here: https://books2read.com/u/mVrGwP

The fantasy romance readers look no further than a **"Red Light District"** a curvy girl, fling romance here: https://books2read.com/u/m2RQ6G

Pressure: Pierce Motors Book 2

Pressure is a hot, enemies-to-lovers romance, contemporary romance.....

Falling for her best friend's brother was the worst and best thing Sarai could've done....

Malik Pierce is next in line to become the next CEO for a billion-dollar racing company. His family has groomed him for this position and their high expectations come with the privilege. He should be over the moon but instead the weight of a cheating scandal weighs heavy on his mind and his reputation.

Sarai Lambert left her home town to pursue her career and her dream of finding the right man. Now she's been handed both. Malik is everything she's ever wanted, minus the scandalthat is slandering his name and threatening her dreams.

Can Malik and Sarai find a way to make it work, or will Malik's problems tear them further apart?

WHAT'S NEXT?!

Want to know what happens next?

Follow me on social media to catch the next release.

Reviews are the lifeblood of the publishing world. They're read, appreciated, and needed. Please consider taking the time to leave a few words on Goodreads, or BookBub.

Sign up for updates and sneak peaks at the site below.
https://www.bookbub.com/chiquitadennie
https://www.chiquitadennie.com
https://www.goodreads.com/author/chiquitadennie
https://Facebook.com/chiquitassteamyreadinggroup
x.com/authorchiquitad
https://www.instagram.com/authorchiquitadennie
https://www.Facebook.com/authorchiquitadennie
https://www.304publishing.tumblr.com

Refuel Playlist @304publishing

1. Toni Braxton-You're Making Me High
2. Janet Jackson-Any Time Any Place
3. The Delfinoics-Didn't I Blow Your Mind This Time
4. Michael Bolton-When A Man Loves A Woman
5. Bonnie Raitt-Something to Talk About
6. Justin Timberlake-Rock Your World
7. Alicia Keys-Un-thinkable (I'm Ready)
8. Mya-It's All about Me
9. Foxy Brown-Hot Spot
10. Beyonce-Baby Boy

About the Author

Chiquita Dennie is an author of Contemporary, Romantic Suspense, Erotic, and Women's Fiction.

Chiquita lives in Los Angeles, CA. Before she started writing contemporary romance, she worked in the entertainment industry on notable TV shows such as the Dr. Phil show, the Tyra Banks show, American Idol, and Deal or No Deal. But her favorite job is the one she's now doing: full-time writing romance.

A best-selling author and award-winning filmmaker, her first short film, "Invisible," was released in summer 2017 and screened in multiple festivals and won for Best Short Film. She also hosts a podcast that showcases the latest in beauty, business, and community called "Moscato and Tea." Her debut release of *Antonio and Sabrina Struck in Love* has opened a new avenue of writing that she loves. Nominated for 2021 Author of the Year, Best Black Romance "Mutual Agreement," and Best Interracial Romance for "She's All In Need". In 2022 nominated Author Queen of the Year, Best Black Romance "Nasir" Best Interracial Romance "Torn" and Best Romantic Comedy "Something Gained" by Black Girls Who Write.

If you want to know when the next book will come out, please visit my website at http://www.chiquitaden nie.com, where you can sign up to receive an email for my next release.

Also by Chiquita Dennie

Series

<u>Struck in Love</u>

The Early Years-A Prequel Short Story

Ruthless:Antonio and Sabrina Book 1

Savage: Antonio and Sabrina Book 2

Beastl: Antonio and Sabrina Book 3

Captivated By His Love:Janice and Carlo

Brutal: Antonio and Sabrina Booke 4

Redemption: Antonio and Sabrina Book 5

<u>Heart of Stone</u>

Broken, Book 1 (Emery & Jackson)

A Valentine's Day Short Book 1.5 Emery & Jackson

Rebirth, Book 2 (Jordan and Damon)

Reveal, Book 3 (Angela and Brent)

Bottoms Up Book 3.5 Jessica and Joseph Short

Renew, Book 4 (Jessica and Joseph)

<u>Cocky Billionaire Boys</u>

Cocky Catcher (Cocky Billionaire Boys Book 1)

Bossy Billionaire (Cocky Billionaire Boys Book 2)

<u>The Fuertes Cartel</u>

Stolen (The Fuertes Cartel Book 1)

Saved (The Fuertes Cartel Book 2)

Betrayed (The Fuertes Cartel Book 3)

Carrington Cartel

Torn: The Carrington Cartel Book 1

Claim: The Carrington Cartel Book 2

Something

Something Gained: A Romantic Comedy Book 1

Something Earned: A Romantic Comedy Book 2

Pierce Motors

Refuel:(Pierce Motors Book 1)

Pressure:(Pierce Motors Book 2)

Summer Break

Summer Nights(Summer Break Book 1)

TN Seal Security

Aydin: Book 1

Nasir: Book 2

Nicco: Book 3

Standalones

Until Serena(HEA World Novel)

Temptation

She's All I Need

I Deserve His Love

Mutual Agreement

Scoring with Sadie

Exposed (A Bodyguard Novel)

Love Shorts:A Collection of Short Stories

Red Light District(A Fantasy Romance Short)

By Keke Renée:

Wet Heat

His Peace, Her Pleasure

Baby, It's Cold Outside

Love Don't Live Here Anymore, Book 1, 2

Every Time We Touch (A Wet Heat Novelette)

One Night Only- Love By Design Book 1

Cassian and Savannah Love By Design Book 2

Deidra's Love -Love By Design Book 3

Protecting Bria: Book 1

Protecting Chanel:Book 2

Protecting Yanira: Book 3

Haven: A Single Dad Romance

Sensual

Seek to Please: Book 1

Seek To Touch: Book 2

Seek To Bare:Book 3

Seek To Love: Book 4

Seek To Trust: Book 5

Seek To Earn: Book 6

Tease Me: Book 1

Promise Me: Book 1

By Ava S.King

Fatal Memory: Book 1 Teagan Stone

Fatal Target: Book 2 Teagan Stone

Fatal Crime: Book 3 Teagan Stone

Fatal Justice: Book 4 Teagan Stone

Fatal Enemy: Book 5 Teagan Stone

Fatal Death: Book 6 Teagan Stone

Fatal Revenge: Book 7 Teagan Stone

Fatal Pursuit: Book 8 Teagan Stone

Mirror of Lies: Book 1

Mirror of Lust: Book 2

Ruined: Andi Easton Book 1

Thank you so much for reading and if you enjoyed the crazy ride and decide to leave a review we'd truly appreciate the support..

Acknowledgments

A huge thank you to my team that helps me behind the scenes, from my editors, test readers, graphic designers, and the list goes on. Truly appreciate each of you for keeping me on my toes.

304 Publishing Company

We showcase authors writing Romance, Women's Fiction, Thriller, and Erotic.Along with Mystery, Suspense, Poetry, Beauty, and Style Books. Thank you for taking the time out to visit. Join our mailing list to stay updated with new releases and blog posts.

www.ingramcontent.com/pod-product-compliance
Lightning Source LLC
Chambersburg PA
CBHW010540170726
48285CB00008B/2695